# HER MILLIONAIRE, HIS MIRACLE

BY
MYRNA MACKENZIE

MILLS & BOON®
*Pure reading pleasure*™

First published in Great Britain 2008
Harlequin Mills & Boon Limited,
Eton House, 18-24 Paradise Road, Richmond, Surrey TW9 1SR

© Myrna Topol 2008

ISBN: 978 0 263 20363 9

Set in Times Roman 10½ on 12¾ pt
07-0908-48007

Printed and bound in Great Britain
by Antony Rowe Ltd, Chippenham, Wiltshire

**Myrna Mackenzie** is a self-proclaimed 'student of all things that concern women and their relationships'. An award-winning author of over thirty novels, Myrna was born in a small town in Dunklin County, Missouri, grew up just outside Chicago, and now divides her time between two lake areas, both very different and both very beautiful. She loves coffee, hiking, cruising the internet for interesting websites and 'attempting' gardening, cooking and knitting. Readers (and other potential gardeners, cooks, knitters, writers, etc...) can visit Myrna online at www.myrnamackenzie.com, or write to her at PO Box 225, La Grange, IL 60525, USA.

# CHAPTER ONE

*TURN around. Go back home. This could all go so wrong. What was I thinking when I decided to go through with this?* Eden Byars tried to appear calm as the housekeeper at Oak Shores showed her into Jeremy Fulton's north suburban Chicago mansion, but her thoughts didn't seem to be willing to play the game.

*Just keep moving forward,* she ordered herself. This was too great an opportunity. She couldn't let old, uncomfortable memories mess things up.

"Excuse me?" the housekeeper asked.

Eden blinked. Had she spoken her thoughts out loud? Maybe. "The house is beautiful," she said, trying to regain her poise. "I'd forgotten." And she had never actually been inside. Not even inside the gates or down the long, winding drive shaded by oaks. In fact, she'd only ever seen glimpses of the imposing mansion in the winter when the leaves had fallen.

The woman tilted her head. "Yes, there's no other like it. Mr. Fulton is in the library, right through there. He's expecting you." She indicated a massive set of mahogany doors and left to return to her duties.

Eden stood before the doors, smoothing her hands over her

old navy-blue skirt. Silly to be nervous. She'd barely known Jeremy ten years ago. They'd hardly exchanged a dozen words beyond hello and goodbye. Different social classes, different everything. It had been a nonexistent relationship.

Except for the fact that she'd had an overwhelming secret and painful crush on him until...

Eden's face grew warm with embarrassment. She took a deep breath.

*Dusty history, Byars. He won't remember. Please.* And even if he did, it couldn't matter. She had to have the job she'd heard Jeremy was trying to fill. Fate had thrown her a curve last month just when she thought she was back on her feet. Suddenly she was down on her luck again. Creditors were calling and all of her plans were on the brink of evaporating if she didn't do something quickly.

A sick feeling slipped into her stomach. The thought of standing before Jeremy and revealing her desperation while he judged her brought back old flashbacks from high school of never fitting in.

But that had been long ago. Awkwardness was no longer her constant companion. She'd changed.

Apparently, so had Jeremy. In one major way.

Eden closed her eyes, remembering what she'd heard. She tried not to think of how he'd once been with that disarming amber gaze and those wild, reckless ways that made girls forgive him anything. Fast and brilliant and very openly temporary, he had been the most vital, alive male she'd ever known.

And now he was...

Eden backed away from the thought. *Don't think about it. I can handle this,* she told herself.

Could she? Maybe. Yes. She had to. Jeremy's situation wasn't her concern. No man was, not in a personal way. Besides, he was no longer a boy she coveted. He was just a man with a job to fill, someone who could aid or ruin her, and loitering outside the library wasn't helping things. If she didn't prove to Jeremy that she was the best—a term no one would have tagged her with when she was younger—if she didn't convince him to hire her…

*I'll lose everything I've worked for.* The distant dreams that had kept her going this past year would never materialize.

"I won't let that happen," she whispered. Not again. Ignoring her pounding heart and a lot of unfortunate memories, Eden took a deep breath, pushed at the massive mahogany door and prepared to confront her past.

Jeremy rose from the desk where he'd been sitting when the door opened. His housekeeper had buzzed him to let him know Eden was here several minutes ago and he'd been wondering why she hadn't appeared yet.

Well, sort of wondering. He imagined it took a bit of courage to face an old acquaintance under these circumstances. But he refused to examine his circumstances. Too many dangerous emotions down that path, something he'd learned to avoid. Instead he concentrated on the moment…and the woman. He would have preferred someone who'd never known him as he once had been, but Eden had been sent here by her cousin, Ashley, an old friend of his whom he trusted implicitly.

He looked toward Eden, turning his head slightly to catch the best possible view of her. It was a habit he'd had to get used to of late, and it worked, albeit imperfectly.

*Showtime, Fulton. Put the big smile on for the lady.* Skirting the desk's perimeter, he moved toward Eden with the skill of recent practice and years of athleticism.

"Eden, it's good to see you," he said, focusing on the striking, slender woman. She seemed different, more vibrant than he remembered, and he didn't think it was just a trick of his vision. When they'd been in high school, he would catch glimpses of her in the hallway, and though she had been pretty with her big gray eyes and long brown hair, she'd always had a scared, shy look about her.

Poised in his doorway, however, Eden didn't radiate shyness. The details might be fuzzy but he could tell her chin was raised. There was determination in her demeanor. Small and delicate as she was, she still faced him boldly. That determination turned a girl who had once been merely pretty into someone much more arresting, Jeremy thought with sudden awareness.

"You're looking well, Jeremy," she said in a low, pleasant and intriguingly soft voice. Only her head drooped slightly before she forced it back up.

Touché, Jeremy thought, catching that slight movement. She knew his situation and she was determined to tough it out and pretend that nothing was wrong with him.

He stepped closer and took a deep breath. Might as well wade in. Anyone who took on this job would have to face some difficult situations, possibly some uncomfortable conversations. It was time to begin the assessment in earnest.

"The Eden I once knew would never have been bold enough to tell me that I was looking well," he suggested, dropping his voice slightly.

Eden stilled as if uncertain how to react, but she raised

her chin still higher. "The Eden you once knew doesn't exist any longer."

He nodded, even though he didn't totally believe her. Everyone carried around pieces of their old selves. He certainly did.

"Well then, welcome, to the new Eden." Jeremy held out his hand. She placed hers in it. Ever so briefly, he wrapped his fingers around hers. His awareness of her as a woman deepened, but he didn't let it show. When he'd been young, his anger at his fate and his spiteful guardian aunt had led him into deliberately reckless behavior that won the admiration of his peers and sent his aunt into a rage. But even then, he'd never involved innocents like Eden in his games. Shy, impoverished females had offered risks he hadn't wanted to deal with.

They still did, and now, more than ever, he tried to control his emotions. *Never reveal weakness, never get close to anyone* had always been the code he lived by. These days, with his future too complicated and uncertain to even consider getting involved with a woman, his physical reaction to Eden was a sure sign that he should send her away. Still, he had promised Ashley he would give her cousin a fair chance.

"Why don't you have a seat and we'll talk." He gestured toward a bank of sofas, then kept a distance behind Eden as she moved toward them. She was compact and slim, and her movements were graceful. He frowned at the fact that he had been unable to keep from noticing that. The way Eden looked when she moved had nothing to do with this job.

Jeremy pushed his reaction aside. He rested his hips against a cherrywood sideboard that dated to colonial times. "Ashley's a skilled human resources representative, and she believes that you're the best person for the job I'm trying to fill."

"Yes, I know. And I've always respected her opinions."

Jeremy couldn't help smiling at the audacity of her statement. Had she blushed when she said that? He couldn't be certain. Colors were getting to be a problem, but he was almost certain that she had blushed.

Interesting. Remembering that younger, shyer Eden, he wondered how much of her assertiveness was an act. The job in question dealt with sensitive issues, and the person he hired had to be just right. He wished he could read her expression better, but there were only six feet between them and at such close range the angle was wrong. Her face wasn't in focus.

Frustration boiled up, but he carefully tamped it down. His limitations weren't her fault.

"Ashley led me to believe that you'd welcome this position despite the fact that neither she nor you knows more than the basic requirements and none of the details. Forgive me, but while that tells me that you need the work, this is a special job. It requires honesty and trust, and I have to know exactly who I'm hiring. Despite growing up near each other and having a passing acquaintance, you and I don't have enough of a history for me to offer you the position without knowing more about you than I already do."

And there it was. For the first time Eden looked gen-uinely flustered and nervous. Her hands clutched at her skirt, tightening on the cloth. Even he could see that sudden telling movement. Still, despite the way she suddenly shifted in her seat and the deep, audible breath she took, she stared directly at him. "I'm afraid what little you know of me isn't particularly complimentary. Our past association…at least that one day…was something I've regretted."

Eden's voice wobbled slightly, but she held his gaze, dropping that live-ember confession into the conversation. Suddenly the tension rolled in, the past stepped into the present and the elephant he'd been ignoring so far ran loose in the library. Jeremy knew exactly what Eden was referring to. On a day long ago, just before he'd left for college, he had come across her bent over her dog, which had died. Jeremy didn't remember much about the poor animal except that it had been gray with age. What he remembered was how Eden had looked as if she was unaware of who and what he was for the first time. She had launched her delicate little grief-racked body against him. He remembered how she had held on and clutched at him as he had done what would surely have been natural for anyone in such a situation. Without even thinking, he had placed his arms around her and held her as she had sobbed out her misery. And then, when her last sobs had faded away, she had lifted her tear-streaked face, wrapped her thin arms around his neck and kissed him—a hot, hard and fervently awkward kiss.

His body had instantly responded to the feel of warm, female flesh against his, but some shred of decency had kicked in. Given the situation, he had simply held on and let her kiss him, and soon she had pulled back, her lashes drooping with embarrassment as she stumbled and ran away. Three weeks later he had headed off to Yale and had not seen her since.

Now he relived that moment. She was apologizing, Jeremy realized, trying to clear the air, scrub the past away and move beyond it. Under the circumstances, a gentleman would probably pretend he had no memory of the incident, but if he ended up hiring Eden, he would have to share his own terrible secrets. There would have to be a great degree of trust between them. Pretending ignorance wasn't an option.

"What was your dog's name?" he asked gently.

"Elton," she answered without hesitation. Then she turned her head for a moment as if gathering her thoughts before facing him again. "I meant it when I said that I'm no longer the same person I once was," she said. "I doubt it was a secret that I had a huge crush on you. Every girl did, but that won't be a problem now. I'm no longer starry-eyed, and I'm not looking for a white knight to save me.

"In fact, for reasons of my own, I'm not interested in even the possibility of a relationship anymore, so if you hire me you won't have to worry about me getting all dreamy-eyed or running into walls whenever you're around, Jeremy. Or…or trying to kiss you again."

Just like that, sudden heat slipped through Jeremy's body. He ignored it. "It wasn't exactly a hardship having you kiss me, Eden, but you're right. This would be a different kind of relationship. You would be my employee. I wouldn't expect physical contact and I wouldn't try to kiss you, either."

She froze. He saw that much. "No, of course not," she said. "Jeremy, I'm only here because I need and want work. I'm here because Ashley thought I could help. I *do* have significant skills to offer."

Jeremy studied her for a moment, his admiration

growing. Eden was still tense. Even with his poor vision, he could see her fingers curling and uncurling against her skirt. Yet she sat tall and straight and proud. She wasn't running, despite her discomfort.

"You don't really even know what the facts surrounding this job are yet," he said.

"No, I don't. I'll want to know the facts, of course, but I'm assuming you'll tell me what I need to know before either of us has to make a decision." The visual details of those gray eyes were indistinct, but Jeremy could nonetheless feel Eden's gaze resting on him. He breathed in deeply and caught a hint of a violetlike scent. No doubt it was the gathering darkness of his condition that forced him to rely on cues other than vision, but he was aware of Eden in a way he never had been. There was almost an electric hum buzzing between them, as if some primal toggle switch had been turned on that long-ago day when they touched, and he was now having difficulty turning it off. That wasn't good, and yet in these few moments he had decided that he was glad she wasn't a total stranger. Pride had gotten him through the worst moments of his life. He'd kept his secrets locked inside. Now he had even more secrets, and they were too painful and personal to trust to a stranger. The very thought of the situation that had made this job a necessity nearly doubled him over with regret and anger, but he forced himself to somehow keep standing and breathing. He concentrated on Eden, even though concentrating on her offered clear risks.

"I'll tell you what you want to know," he agreed, "before I ask you to take on this task, but I need to ask you some questions first."

Eden nodded, but she looked suddenly wary. She took a deep, audible breath. "All right. Ask. Let's get this party started," she said, then groaned. "I can't believe I actually said that. I'm really not living in a time warp."

But the tension that had been ripping through him eased a bit. Jeremy couldn't help chuckling. "Let's just say that you have a good memory, Eden. And that's a good thing. I had almost forgotten how much I used to use that phrase."

Eden fought to keep sitting still. She hadn't realized how difficult it would be to find herself this close to Jeremy. He was more handsome than ever, his amber eyes intent, his chestnut hair sun kissed. He obviously still worked out, from the look of his body. Those broad shoulders and lean hips had raised her temperature all too many times.

Only the way he tilted his head and seemed to focus on some point to one side of her face gave away his situation. And the lines of tension that hadn't been there before. None of that could hide the fact that he was achingly attractive.

And she was apparently lucky that she had remembered that phrase from the past. Back when Jeremy had been young and wild, he had been known to say that frequently, probably to irritate his aunt, from what Ashley had told Eden.

"I guess it was a small detail that stuck in my mind," she said with a shrug.

He nodded. "Details can be important. Very important in some cases. Tell me a few details about yourself."

The intensity with which Jeremy was focusing on her moved up several notches, and Eden's breath stalled in her throat. He had been looking at her all along. Indeed, when she'd made that stupid comment about him not having to worry about her kissing him again, his gaze had locked on her, raising her temperature and her awareness of him as a man. She had cursed herself for even using the word *kiss*. But this was different. Jeremy's concentration seemed to increase a hundredfold. Eden could see why he had been so successful at chasing new clients in the field of technology if he went after success with such fervor. It felt as if he was concentrating his whole being on her, as if every cell in his body was waiting for her response.

She had to ignore that if she was going to keep breathing and functioning normally. She couldn't go silent and shy now.

"I'm not sure what Ashley told you, but as a teacher in a private school in St. Louis, I have my summers free," she managed to say. "I'm available until the end of August."

Incredibly available. Six weeks ago her car had conked out and had to be replaced. Then, when her school had been forced to make cuts last month, she'd kept her job but lost all her extracurricular positions. The largest and last of the huge debts her ex-husband had left her with still had to be paid off, and the creditors were growing impatient. All her second chances were gone. With this job, she could get free. Without it, she was staring at bankruptcy.

But as Jeremy nodded, Eden didn't get the impression that her answer about her schedule had made much of an impact. Ashley had probably already explained all of this to him. She still hadn't convinced him.

Jeremy straightened to his full height, moved away from the sideboard and took a few steps closer. An errant lock of that chestnut hair fell over his forehead, and Eden felt an urge to lick her lips, to shift nervously in her chair, to get up and pace the room. Instead, she carefully folded her hands in her lap and waited.

"Ashley told me that you raised your siblings almost single-handedly."

Blinking, Eden forgot to be nervous for a second. He hadn't known that? But no, why should he have? Just because he had been Ashley's friend hadn't meant that he would have been privy to her cousin's private information. "Yes. My parents divorced early and my uncle, Ashley's father, let us live in a building on his property, so we had a roof over our heads, but my mother was frequently ill." Her mother had been an alcoholic before her death last year. She had been loving but mostly unavailable.

"So between your job and your personal life, you've had a great deal of experience with children and parents." Jeremy was studying her more closely now, his expression more intense.

"Yes, of course." Eden frowned. "I'm afraid...I don't understand. Ashley told me that you had a short-term project, but these references to children...do you have a child you need me to care for?" She supposed it was possible. Jeremy had surely made love to a number of women, she knew, trying not to conjure up the image of a passionate and naked Jeremy. He might have conceived a child.

"Forgive me, Eden. Just a few more questions. Then, if we're in agreement, I'll explain," he said, his expression gentling.

She understood. If they weren't in agreement, he would send her home and she would never have any idea what this was about. She would go home empty-handed. "All right," she said around the nervous lump in her throat.

A few seconds of silence followed. Jeremy tented his fingers. "If you had to deliver bad news to a child or that child's parents, do you feel confident that you could do so in a tactful manner? And…I don't mean to insult you in any way, but could you promise that whatever news you were privy to would go no further than the primary parties involved?"

Eden nearly laughed at that. She had spent years explaining her mother's lapses and absences to her sisters. Plus… "Jeremy, I'm a teacher. Delivering less than positive news is part of the job. I work hard at letting people down gently during those occasions when disappointing news has to be conveyed. As to your second concern, confidentiality is a given in my profession. I deal with touchy issues on a regular basis. Abuse, abandonment, learning disabilities, psychological problems. I would never discuss those situations outside the bounds of the primary parties. I would never betray a child or that child's parents." She searched her mind for proof. Words were so easy. They could be so unconvincing. "I never told anyone about the car," she said softly.

Jeremy's intensity eased slightly. He laughed. "You slid that into the conversation pretty smoothly."

"You hadn't forgotten?"

"Eden, a man doesn't forget when he totals an Aston Martin. It's a life-changing event. I wasn't even supposed to be driving that car. It was my aunt's favorite. Practically a family member to her. And while I never liked the woman and she detested me, even so…what a jerk I was." He shook his head. "And no, I guess you never did tell, because when I came out of the coma two days after the accident, everyone assumed that it was another driver's fault that I hit that stop sign."

"It *was* another driver's fault in a way. You did swerve to avoid hitting him."

Jeremy shook his head. "But if I hadn't foolishly taken my eyes off the road to wave at you, I would have seen the car and slowed. I wouldn't have had to swerve."

Eden inwardly cringed at the fact that he had seen her that day. Her uncle had forced her to wear a hideous, orange-and-red-flowered dress from a charity basket—to show her gratitude for the gift, he had said—and she hadn't wanted Jeremy to see her in it. When she had seen his car, she had tried to hide behind a tree, but she hadn't been fast enough. The dress was like a flashing beacon. Their eyes had met. There had been nothing he could do but wave at her.

"Well, you did the right thing in the end," she said. "You told your aunt everything once you were well."

"But you kept my secret," he mused.

"It was *your* secret," she said simply. She meant every word. A girl who grew up with a mother who was unable to be a parent because of her drinking problem knew too well what it was like to have to face humiliating truths. Between that and this last year after her husband's desertion and betrayal, she knew what it was to have things she wanted to hide from the world. "It wasn't mine to tell," she said simply.

"And what if I had hurt others in that accident?"

Eden closed her eyes and looked away. "I would have told, then," she said, guessing that was not the answer he sought.

Silence followed. Somewhere a clock chimed. Eden waited, sure she would be shown the door. The clock chimed again.

"I'm going to tell you a secret, Eden," Jeremy finally said. "And eventually, if you still want the position after you know all that the job entails, then I'm going to hire you. You might regret taking it before the next few weeks are over."

She was regretting it already. From the minute that Ashley had called her, she had regretted even considering coming here, just as she'd known she would take this job despite any regrets.

"Tell me," she said. "Whatever it is that I need to know."

For a second when Jeremy looked toward her, she could swear that he saw her clearly. His expression was that intense. Her heart began to pound. "When I was in college," he began, "I was a sperm donor. My reasons were…not the usual and they weren't honorable. I wasn't in it for the money the way many of the donors were. I wasn't even trying to do something noble by attempting to help another human being. I don't want to go into the details, but let's just say that it was a rash act, and the whole experience was very short term, not nearly as long as the months most donors commit to. Nevertheless, I may have fathered children. I most likely did, even though I have no idea of how many there might be. Not many, I would think, if any. Still…" His jaw hardened.

"I—" Eden's heart pounded even harder. She didn't know where this was going, but she could tell that it was going somewhere bad.

He held up one hand, stopping her speech.

"Eden, it's important that I find any children I may have fathered. I have good reasons, not frivolous ones, and I need…"

She looked up, straight into his anguished eyes. "It's because you're going blind. You're afraid for them," she said.

"Yes." He bit off the word harshly.

"The sperm bank?"

"Out of business. I've hired a private investigator to help out, but once that bridge is crossed, there will need to be personal contact. Interaction. I'll want to help anyone affected, to refer them to those who can advise them, to provide money and care if the worst comes to pass. I'll want them to know what to expect. I have to do this right. Those children and their parents have to be protected. They have to be approached with sensitivity, more than I trust myself to be capable of."

She stood and moved closer. The desire to touch him was strong, but she wouldn't do that.

"Tell me what they can expect. What can you do? What can you see?"

He turned and looked down at her, and now, with only a small bit of space separating them, she realized the full impact of being this close to him.

"I can't do everything I used to do, but I do all that I can," he said quietly. "And I can still see you. At least for now. I can still see most of you."

Eden's breathing kicked up. She had no idea what "most of you" meant, but the mere fact that he was concentrating on her with such fierceness made her heart race.

"You're good with children?" he asked.

"Yes. Very good. My students are happy. My sisters, whom I raised, don't live near but they call frequently."

"You care about young people, then. You can talk to them and their families."

He was closer still. Somehow she managed to nod. "I can do that."

"When the time comes," he continued. "When I find them—and I will—I'll need someone who understands the complexities and fears and joys of children. I have no experience and I won't have any. There'll be no children for me. I won't risk passing this on to anyone else, but for anyone who might share my DNA I'll do what I can. I'll want you to help me research the possibilities for maintaining normalcy from those who've lived through it, not just from my doctors. I'll want you to help me be an example of what can be, not what can't be. Do you understand, Eden?"

She understood that this man fought demons, that he was racked with guilt, that he had closed off avenues in his future. She also understood what he was asking her and what taking this position might cost her, because he was just as potent as ever.

"I understand. I'm not only an excellent teacher, by the way. I'm an excellent researcher. And I have contacts. People who work with those in need. Discreet people. I know that's not what you were asking, but it might help you…and in helping you be a help to the children. I think you need the skills I possess."

He stood there for a minute as if astonished at her words.

"I think Ashley might have been right." Jeremy reached out as if to touch her before lowering his hand to his side. But despite his failure to make contact, her body jolted. For a long moment she was too aware of herself as a woman and Jeremy as a man she had once longed for desperately. That was so wrong and emotionally dangerous, and every fiber of her being told her to run. Now. Before she got hurt.

The men who'd had had the greatest impact on her life,

from her worthless, absent father to her resentful, unloving uncle to her faithless, undependable husband, had only ever brought pain and humiliation into her life. And those had been men she at least had something in common with, not someone like Jeremy, who inhabited a world that didn't even intersect with her own. So no, she couldn't risk her heart and dignity again.

Except…she would. Her financial situation was so dire that she couldn't even consider walking away. And the children facing a frightening future…she couldn't ignore them, could she?

"Here are the details of your employment," he told her, and he named a sum of money that nearly made Eden's head spin. "That as well as room and board. Can you get me started on the path I need to follow? Will you stay with me until this is done or until the summer ends?" he asked.

There had been a time when she would have given all that she was to hear Jeremy ask if she would stay with him, but that had been a young girl's dream. A shimmery, no-connection-to-reality dream that was, thankfully, long gone. This was entirely different. It was real, and it was simply work, she told herself.

"I'll stay," she promised. Just to help and to work, she reminded herself again.

"Good," Jeremy said with a sudden brilliant smile that turned him into pure male temptation. Eden wanted to groan. "You've made me a happy man."

The comment made Eden wonder how many women Jeremy had said that to and under what circumstances, and she knew then how risky this situation was. The fact that she was even wondering about Jeremy's love life meant that she was just as susceptible to Jeremy's charms as she had always been.

But she had no choice. *And this time I'm not giving in to temptation,* she told herself. *That's a stone-solid promise.* And she always kept her promises.

## CHAPTER TWO

"I'D LIKE you to start immediately just in case the private investigator turns in some results soon," Jeremy said. "Since you're not from the area, I've taken the liberty of having the guest house readied."

"You were that sure I would suit and that I would take the job?"

He laughed. He hadn't been sure of anything and still wasn't. "The guest house had been allowed to fall into a state of disrepair. It needed work, anyway. Come on, I'll take you there."

Automatically he held out one hand for hers and dropped a pair of sunglasses on his nose with the other. Then he smiled.

She hesitated, then took his hand. Heat flowed from her fingers to his. He ignored it.

"I'll lead," he told her just in case she thought that by taking her by the hand he had been asking her to help him. Pride had been his lifelong companion. It had made life with a dysfunctional past and a guardian who despised him bearable. And pride didn't allow pity.

"I'll follow," she agreed, and as he let go of her, she dutifully did just that. They traveled in silence across the broad expanse of lawn that he'd covered so many times in his youth that the path was emblazoned on his brain.

When the first fuzzy outlines of the house came into sight he heard her gasp.

"It's small," he explained. "Only three rooms. My aunt didn't particularly care for guests."

"The size doesn't matter. It's gorgeous, cozy and such detail!" Then her voice tailed off. He knew what she was thinking.

"Don't do that, Eden. No, I can't make out all the small stuff these days, but if you're going to spend a lot of time trying to spare my feelings or worrying over every word you say, I'm going to be sorry we decided to work together."

"Maybe I wasn't worried about your feelings but about my own for saying what might have been misconstrued. I'm supposed to be aware of the situation and in control if I'm going to be able to help you. At all times. But I spoke without even thinking. That isn't allowed. At least not in my book."

"Nice save," he said with a smile. "You *are* professional."

She hesitated. "Thank you," she said primly.

Which only made him want to smile more. "Give yourself a chance," he told her. "I've had months to get used to this and to learn everything I needed to know. This is all new to you. It'll take some time. And yes, the cottage does have very nice details," he said, moving up the three steps to the small porch. "A spindlework beaded frieze over the porch, a patterned gable with a finial on top, fish-scale shingles. It's definitely a textured house."

And textures, touching, which had always been important to him, had taken on a new importance these days.

He had stopped at the right angle so that he caught part of her smile. "What?" he asked.

She shook her head. "Nothing. It's just that this doesn't seem like a house that you would own."

He lifted his left eyebrow, wondering where this was leading. "Why not?"

"I don't know. I picture you in either something horribly elegant the way the mansion is or else in something terribly masculine, all stone and massive timbers. This house is…"

"Too pretty with all that china-blue and lacy-white paint? Too fussy?"

She laughed, and it was such a lovely, foreign sound that he wondered if he had ever heard her laugh before.

"Not fussy. Cozy," Eden corrected, "but yes, it's a bit of a Hansel-and-Gretel gingerbread of a house. A fairy-tale house. You sound as if you have some affection for it."

Jeremy shrugged. "It made a good hideout for me when I was growing up."

"I'll bet your friends loved it."

"You might say that." He had mostly brought girls here. They hadn't noticed the details, and he hadn't pointed them out, but he had no intention of mentioning that to Eden. There was already too much electricity arcing between them.

"I'll have one of my employees bring in your bags. You'll want to have some time to yourself." He moved down the stairs and away. "The place is open right now, but the keys are on the kitchen table. Use them. This is a safe neighborhood, but I don't believe in taking chances." Not anymore.

"Jeremy?"

He stopped and turned.

She frowned. "Until there are some children and parents to talk to, what do you want me to do?"

*Come closer,* automatically came to mind, followed immediately by *Don't come closer.* "Prepare yourself," he said, instead. "Read up on my condition and the risks inherent to any children I might have fathered so that you'll be able to understand and explain it to those you'll need to talk to. I have plenty of material in the library as well as banks of computers. I'll show you after dinner. For now, just get your bearings and the lay of the land."

She furrowed her brow. "That's all? That is, I'm a good researcher and I'm sure that will take *some* time but…you're paying me well. Isn't there anything else I can do?"

Jeremy blew out a breath and thought about the fact that a few years ago he would never have believed he would have a need to hire Eden at all. Now she was a necessity, and the reason for that was too unnerving, frustrating and despair making.

He slowly shook his head and felt the slick slide of regret and anger push at him from all sides, but he battled it into simmering submission. He had to, because if he didn't, his anger might show. It might come bubbling out, and it wasn't Eden that he was angry with, but life, and his life was not her fault. For once, it wasn't even his fault.

Carefully he searched for the words to explain. "I'm sure you know this, Eden, because you grew up in this area, but I have servants who clean and keep my house and who cook for me. I have gardeners and accountants. Those people have always been a part of my life, and the only new people I've hired are the investigator and you. He's investigating. You're…getting ready and waiting. The getting ready is really important, but it's the afterward that's most important. So, the answer is no on having other work for you. Other than what I've told you, you can't help me. You *really* can't help me," he repeated.

His words and his tone had come out too harsh, and Eden was looking wary. "I didn't mean to appear flippant," she said.

He held up a hand to stop her. "I didn't think you were being flippant. But, this situation…" He blew out a breath. "The situation is this. You're here because there may be a child or children who need your help. If I could go back and change the past, I would never have risked fathering a child, but it *is* the children I'm asking for your help with, and…I'm not a child."

"I know that."

"You don't. Not in the sense that I mean. You see a man disintegrating from what he was, one no longer as capable as he once was. You see a need and you want to help. That's…nice, but understand that that kind of help isn't what I need."

She stood there, silent, tension hanging in the air. "What do you need?"

*To be whole, to be a complete man, to rewrite the past and change the future.* "Why does it matter?"

"Your needs will be *their* needs if the worst comes to pass," she said simply. "Isn't that important?"

"Yes." But conceding that was getting too close to admitting things he wasn't prepared to admit yet. Not to anyone other than himself.

"Besides," she said, taking a step closer and standing

taller. "I won't lie to you. I need this job. I have plans and goals, but before I can make those plans a reality…"

She looked uncomfortable.

"Eden?"

An audible sigh escaped her. "My husband emptied our bank accounts when he left me. He owed money, and I was the one who had to pay the bills. I'm still working on that."

"I see. I could help you."

"No." She shook her head vehemently. "I've already done the dependence routine too many times, and it's a really ugly feeling. I need to take care of this on my own. I can't take unmerited help. I just…I earn my way, and I don't take money I haven't worked for."

"And you feel that's what I'm asking you to do?"

"Yes. In a way."

"What way?"

"In the way people used to act when I lived here. Almost everyone in the area is rich and they all knew that we weren't. They would give us the clothes and furniture they didn't want anymore. I know their intentions were good, but we went to school with their sons and daughters, and taking their charity made us feel as if we were lacking in some way. Equality wasn't possible."

"And you want to be my equal?"

Oh, that definitely was a blush spreading up from the neckline of her white blouse. This time he saw the contrast for certain, and what that did to his imagination was…intriguing and disturbingly erotic.

But Eden had crossed her arms. "I *am* your equal." She said it boldly, even though there was a noticeable tremble in her voice as if she didn't believe her own words.

What could he do? He tilted his head. "Agreed. Absolutely."

She waited. "Work?" she asked.

He searched his mind, then turned his head to the side. "All right, I do have an extra job you can do to earn your keep, since you insist I'm overpaying you."

"You *are* overpaying me. Even a rich boy like you knows that."

"A rich boy?" He couldn't help the mock-indignant look that turned into a smile.

"It's what you are and always have been," she told him. "You wanted me to be truthful."

"But not brutal," he said, intending to tease.

Instantly those crossed arms dropped. "I'm sorry."

"I was kidding. I know what I am, Eden. I'm what you said, and I don't apologize for it."

She nodded. "Don't apologize. You got me through a lot of tough days when I was young."

"I did?"

Her chest rose deliciously. "Yes, you were the fantasy boy girls daydreamed about at school, but don't let it go to your head. I was young and stupid then."

"And now you're not."

"And now I'm definitely not. No more fantasy men in my life. Not even you."

He couldn't help grinning. Was that an answering grin on her face? "Well, it's good that we've established the fact that you're impervious to my wealth and my charming ways."

"We have." But as he stood there gazing her way, charmed by this new impertinent Eden, she took a slight step back. "Now about the extra work…"

Oh yes. Reality. "I'm a computer consultant. I spend all my time with the newest toys in the business," he told her, "but I haven't gotten around to researching the toys that will make those children's lives easier if they should need that kind of help. Oh, I know the possibilities, but there's been no hands-on stuff. I haven't actually tried any of the available tools."

"Because you see well enough."

"Well enough," he agreed. And because he wasn't ready yet to give up even a centimeter he didn't have to, but…

"The children might need some of this stuff. If you could read up, order some samples, try things out…"

"I can do that. And if I need you?"

He couldn't help blinking.

"As a guinea pig, I mean," she explained.

*No,* he wanted to say, but then he was the one who had suggested the task and he really did want to understand the results for the sake of his offspring if he had any.

"If it proves necessary," he finally said, and he took a step closer and took her hand. "Thank you, Eden, for offering to do what I hadn't even asked. You're…very different from what I remember."

He was too close for details but he could tell she was smiling. "You don't really remember much of me," she accused. "Truthfully."

What could he say? Jeremy shrugged. "Truthfully, I don't remember much."

"You were pretty busy in those days."

"I was self-absorbed."

"That, too."

He chuckled. "Maybe I shouldn't have asked for truthfulness."

"I would have given it to you, anyway. I need truth in my life now."

Jeremy nodded. He released her hand, because the truth was that standing this close to her made him remember one thing. She had kissed him once. Obviously, it wasn't going to happen again. She clearly regretted that first time, and given their situation, he knew it would be the worst kind of idea for them to touch.

Still, he'd never been the type to deny himself pleasure just because it was a bad idea. He definitely was attracted to Eden Byars with her clean violet scent, her soft skin and her pretty laugh. He had an aching hunger to feel her lips against his. Just a quick taste. But that was one bit of truth he wasn't offering up. There were some things a man couldn't fight, but sexual temptation could be easily overcome. He wasn't going to touch this woman.

As promised, an employee, Donald, had brought Eden's bags in. "Anything else you need, ma'am?"

She needed him to stop calling her ma'am and looking at her as if she were nobility when she was probably no wealthier than he was. Eden shook her head. "Thank you, no. I appreciate you carrying my things in and taking care of my car."

"Mr. Fulton says that you're to change or pack away anything in the house that doesn't suit you. He had it restored to the way it was years ago, but it's yours while you're here."

"I'm sure it's fine."

Donald nodded. "Sometimes Lula comes in and leaves a few things." His tone was casual but vaguely uncomfortable.

Eden blinked. "Lula?" Was this house where Jeremy brought his women friends?

"Lula's the cook. She was here when Mr. Fulton was young, and when his aunt would get mad at Mr. Fulton—which apparently was a lot—the woman would throw away his stuff. Lula salvaged some of the things and hid them here. She put them away when they were fixing the house, but lately she's been bringing things back piece by piece." Donald smiled.

Eden practically groaned. Not only was she working for Jeremy and living on his property, she was staying in his childhood hideaway surrounded by his boyhood treasures.

"I'm sure everything will be fine. I'm not planning on settling in for very long," she told Donald and herself. "I just—Mr. Fulton just has a job for me to do," she finished lamely, not knowing how much, if anything, Jeremy's servants knew about why she was here. Clearly Ashley hadn't known about the possibility of children.

"It's okay. We know it has something to do with Mr. Fulton not seeing as well as he used to. We know about that, but we don't talk. He really doesn't like people to know." Donald looked at her pointedly, as if to warn her.

Eden didn't know whether to be insulted that Jeremy's servants were issuing not-so-veiled warnings to her, touched that they cared about him that much or alarmed that she felt a rather childish urge to cross her heart and hope to die before she revealed Jeremy's secrets.

"Some things are just off-limits," she said, which pretty much summed up her feelings about the whole situation and seemed to satisfy Donald. She wasn't going to discuss Jeremy with anyone. She didn't even want to think about

Jeremy, and she absolutely did not want to explore her feelings about the day and this necessary but emotionally dangerous situation she was in.

But when Donald had gone and Eden wandered inside, she was pleasantly surprised. She wasn't sure what she'd expected to find, but there weren't any visible traces of Jeremy. Just beautiful, old cottage-style furniture in cream and gold and cornflower-blue. Very comfortable and tasteful. Better quality than anything she had ever owned or ever would own but still homey.

This is nice, she thought, until she opened a drawer on the nightstand and found a stack of old photos. Women. Well, much-younger women, that is. Many she recognized. Rich, gorgeous, the cream of the area. She knew what these were. Mementoes that had been given to Jeremy a long time ago. There was Lara Pettison wearing a skimpy skirt and a midriff top, grinning at the camera as if her expression was all for Jeremy. There was Mindy Tarrant in her cheerleading outfit with "Love ya, Jer. Really!" written on the border in purple ink with a purple kiss drawn next to the writing. For half a second, Eden was back in school, watching Jeremy walk away with a girl who wasn't her. In the next second she wondered if Jeremy knew these were here. She felt like some kind of icky voyeur.

"Does it matter?" she asked herself. "None of this has anything to do with you or your work." Searching around for a box, she laid the photos carefully inside, then put it in the closet and closed the lid. There. She felt a childish sense of satisfaction, as if she had managed to put Jeremy in a box at last.

Maybe she had.

But in the next moment she heard sounds outside and looked out her open window. Jeremy was running past, a pair of runner's shorts revealing strong, muscled thighs. His chest was bare. His broad shoulders glistened with sweat. He gave a quick wave but kept going.

As she watched him moving away, Eden's heart raced. Had she really thought she could ever be completely immune to this man's physical appeal? What woman could?

Her next thought was that she wondered that he could run, given his situation, but he appeared to be doing just that. And moving quickly, too. She remembered him telling her that he did all he could though his sight was failing.

*Reckless,* she thought. *Driven. Still wild. Still dangerous.*

Tomorrow she was going to attack her work with a vengeance. *She* was going to do all that *she* could. Staying here too long couldn't be good for her. She was, literally, sleeping in Jeremy's bed, and the very thought made her tremble.

"Blinders, Byars," she told herself. "Some people can't handle cigarettes or alcohol or food. You can't seem to choose or handle men very well."

It was time to do what she had learned to do best. Move beyond the bad, threatening things in her life. If she could just survive Jeremy one more time, everything would be fine. Surely she could do that, couldn't she?

*Yes, darn it.* But handling things was easier when a person was fully prepped. Information made good armor, so tomorrow she would go hunting. She hoped she'd find something useful.

# CHAPTER THREE

THE woman was prompt. He had to give her that, Jeremy thought, when he came downstairs for breakfast the next day.

"Ms. Byars is in your library," his housekeeper told him. "She said to let you know that she has questions when you have some time."

He immediately put down his napkin. "Show her in."

In less than a minute, Eden was in the doorway. "Have you eaten?" he asked her. He'd had the cottage stocked.

"Just coffee. I've never been a breakfast person."

Because her family hadn't been able to afford much food when she was younger, he would guess. She still was almost too slender. "Mind if I am?"

She tilted her head inquisitively.

"A breakfast person," he explained.

"Oh. No. This can wait."

He shook his head. "Sit. We'll talk. I have a meeting in an hour."

Immediately Eden moved into the room, but off to one side where his peripheral vision was best, Jeremy couldn't help but notice. The temptation to turn so that he was facing her more directly warred with his need to see her better. He had a strong desire to form a full picture of what Eden looked like now. Which was alarming. Eden might have that cool, forthright exterior, but he sensed emotion and complexity beneath the surface. Given his situation and his priorities, that meant she was one woman he needed to keep in a compartment. Business. All business.

"Sit," he said again, a bit too forcefully.

She sat where he directed her, beside him where Mrs. Ruskin had had the maid put an extra place setting. Some people might think he was being overly personal having her sit next to him rather than across from him, but he hated explaining. He turned to get the best view, focusing his full attention on her.

Her response was immediate. She sat up taller, then went totally still, almost rigid. He got the feeling that while Eden might need this job, she wasn't too thrilled about working with him. He remembered what she'd said about having had a crush on him. No doubt she regretted having admitted that.

"I've been reading," Eden rushed in. "I understand the basics, the fact that this condition usually manifests itself earlier in life than it has with you, the fact that it's genetic and that you have a sensitivity to light and only your peripheral version remains untouched."

Ah, so he didn't have to explain why she was beside him and that he wasn't some lech trying to rub knees with her. And yet…she'd made the comment as if she had read his mind. Had he revealed any emotion? Demonstrated any awkwardness or weakness? If so, he would have to watch that. Visible chinks in the armor were unacceptable.

"That's right. If you were in front of me this close, parts

of you would be blurry, but at this angle I can see that you've pulled your hair back, you have dangling earrings and you're wearing a blouse with contrasting buttons. The top one is open."

Those big gray eyes flew open wide. Jeremy suppressed a smile. "Sorry," he said. "I couldn't help noticing, but I probably shouldn't have mentioned it."

She lifted her chin, her color high. "No, that's all right. It helps me to know what the situation is, and I really do need to understand, but…"

He waited. The tension emanating from her was palpable, practically electric. His fingers itched to touch and soothe. With effort he restrained himself.

"Is that how you're able to run?"

Without thought, he turned toward her even though she blurred a bit more. "Partially, yes. I can see part of the ground and things at the edge. What I can't see is what's too far ahead, but the estate is familiar territory and the grounds are well kept. I don't have to worry about hazards or holes or traffic."

"I've had students who were runners. You have a nice form. I mean—"

He held up his hand to stop her. "I know what you meant. You don't have to watch your words or worry that I'll misread anything you say. I think we've established that whatever lay in our past is in the past and this is just business. While I find you attractive, I'm not going to jump you."

For a second she looked startled. "I never thought you would. And…I wouldn't jump you, either. That is—"

He smiled. "It's okay, Eden."

"Not to me, it isn't. I never stammer anymore. It's unprofessional, and I've trained myself not to. Besides, all I really meant to say was that you could have been a runner on the school team. I can see you're that good."

"No. That wouldn't have happened," he said with a small smile. "I never stuck to anything that long." He'd been too busy causing trouble, but there was no reason to say that. They both knew it.

Eden shifted on the seat beside him. Her prim skirt brushed against his leg. An innocent occurrence that connected them for half a second and sent a current of awareness through him. Quickly she smoothed the cloth away, and he controlled the urge to lean closer. She might project a cool, calm demeanor, but there were still traces of the younger, skittish Eden. She'd obviously been hurt by men, and he was her employer, a man she had a right to trust.

"My troublemaking days are over," he assured her.

"Because of your…"

"My blindness? No. It's because I choose for them to be over." Which implied that he might just as easily choose to start them up again.

She nodded. "What else do you do?" she asked, and he saw then that she had pulled out a pad of paper.

He reached out and gently pulled it away. He took her hand and felt her long, slender fingers in his grasp.

"I'll help you with your research when I can, and I'll even try the instruments out when it's necessary, but don't use me as your model. The things I do—well, it wouldn't be wise to make those kinds of promises to a child or a parent. I don't want to be a role model. That's not me." And never had been.

He felt her tremble and take a deep breath. "You're not still the wild one?" she asked, raising her chin as if daring him to answer.

He laughed and gave her back her hand. "Not as wild as I'd like to be. I'm a businessman these days. Boring."

"We'll see," she said with a smile of her own. "And I won't make any promises I can't keep to a child. I don't like disappointing them."

Something warmed inside him. "Ashley chose well," he said.

She shrugged. "I'm her cousin, and she knew I needed the money."

"No. She's a pro. It's more than that. Despite your situation, she wouldn't have recommended you if you weren't suitable. You care about kids more than the average person, don't you?"

"I don't know about that, but I like them a lot. I even plan to have a few of my own, even without a husband. And I want to start a private school where I can help disadvantaged children and make the ones who never feel special realize their potential. So don't think I won't consider your children's needs first. I'll run everything by you before I make any promises."

*Your children.* Jeremy's breath froze in his throat. He'd never gone so far as to think of them in those terms.

"They're not mine. I don't want to stake a claim on those children or have my own. I wouldn't allow that to happen."

She bit her lip. "I just meant— I spoke without thinking."

Jeremy instantly regretted his knee-jerk reaction. He shook his head. "No, I overreacted. But having a family or children…that's completely out of the picture for me."

Thank goodness Eden had just told him that she intended to have some. Because while he found her desirable and could tell she wasn't immune to him, her need to be a parent threw up an impassable barrier that would keep them apart. That was good. It would make working with her in close quarters much easier.

"Jeremy?"

"If you need anything, just ask," he said. "And if you don't eat and take care of yourself you won't be any good for me or for helping the children." His tone was light, but he meant every word.

Her answering laugh was delicious.

"What?"

"Forgive me, but that was such a pathetic ploy to get me to eat breakfast. I would think that someone who'd been born a rebel would know more about getting a rebellious person to do something," she said, rising.

He followed her up so that they were both standing. "What do you mean?"

She tilted her head. "When you were a kid breaking all the rules, what would someone have to do or say to persuade you to do things their way?"

He knew what she was trying to do. "Nothing would have persuaded me if I really didn't want to do something," he told her in a low, conspiratorial voice.

For half a second she looked disappointed, but then she quickly recovered. "Exactly. And if I don't want to eat breakfast, you can't make me."

He grinned at her.

But Eden was looking aghast. "I didn't mean that to come out the way it did. That sounded childish, didn't it?"

"It's okay, Eden. I know you're new at this rebellion thing. You always did what was expected of you, didn't you?"

She frowned. "Always." And then a triumphant look came over her. "That's why I need to assert myself now and be a bit more forceful." She picked up her pad of paper. "No matter what *you* think the children can and cannot do, I think that matter might be open to speculation. No one should be limited by one person's opinion. Each person is an individual and some can do more than others, right?"

Okay, now he *knew* she was trying to manipulate him, but he couldn't help applauding her tenacity. "I'm sure you're right, Eden," he said.

"Now…what other hobbies do you have besides running?" she asked, fishing a pen from the pocket of her skirt.

Appreciating how a woman looks when she believes she's about to experience something wonderful came to mind.

Irrelevant, he reminded himself. And anyway, she had bested him and deserved to be rewarded for her efforts. "I play basketball when I can get Donald in a free moment," he said, searching around for one of the less challenging of his activities. Nothing where a child would get hurt.

"Basketball? That's wonderful."

"Do you play?"

"No. I'm afraid I've never been good at anything physical."

If he'd been drinking coffee he would have choked. As it was, she was the one who looked flustered.

"I mean, I never played sports in school."

"Then you might have a talent for the physical that you haven't discovered," he said.

She looked up at him, blushing furiously. "I might, but

I probably won't find out. Too busy. Work to do." And she scooted away, headed for his library.

Jeremy wondered which one of them had won that bout, but then he shook his head. Maybe both of them had won. Somehow he had managed not to touch her. Which was, of course, a good thing.

Eden carefully closed the library door behind her, then shut her eyes and slid to the floor. Her heart was racing faster than the winner of the Kentucky Derby. That interlude with Jeremy, all that sparring had been…

*Invigorating, exciting.* "Dead wrong," she muttered. He was her boss, not some teenage fantasy crush she was still nurturing. And yet, when he had held her hand, it had been all she could do to sit still. She probably shouldn't have challenged him. She was out of her league. With Jeremy, and in this town, she had *always* been out of her league.

*But at least I got him to help me.* She looked down at the almost-empty sheet of paper. Only one item was listed, but she had added to the knowledge she'd need to help any children. From here on out, she was going to absorb as much as she could by observing Jeremy.

Because while she wanted to escape the crushing weight of debt, the bad memories of this town and the all-too-potent aura of the man, she also did care about the children she would be responsible for guiding into a possibly new and scary life. She really did need to look at things from all angles, and that meant studying the man who was a walking laboratory for her research.

Maybe that was how she should think of him. An experiment, a laboratory subject. But then she thought of his skin against hers when his hand had closed over her fingers and how she had had to look up into those dimming but still-fierce eyes, and everything in her world seemed to narrow to him and her and—

"Okay, not a lab experiment. A man who, unfortunately, makes you hot." One it was dangerous to stare at too much.

"Too bad, Byars," she told herself. She had signed on the dotted line. Jeremy Fulton was hers to watch. For now.

# CHAPTER FOUR

IT HAD been a reasonably successful week, Jeremy tried to tell himself as he shuffled papers at his desk. The private investigator had met with him and Eden and had reported that he had located a former employee of the sperm bank and hoped to be able to finagle a lead out of that. In addition, Jeremy's business was going as well as it always had.

So, it wasn't business that was bothering him right now. It wasn't even his blindness, at least no more than usual.

It was Eden. All week she'd been there in the background like a mouse waiting for a bit of cheese to drop. She'd had her notebook held tightly against her chest like a shield, and she'd tried her best to fade into the background. No doubt she thought she'd succeeded.

*Because I don't see well* was his first angry thought. But he knew it wasn't that. She just thought…he suspected she'd always thought that she was an invisible person, the kind a man didn't notice.

To his shame, he had to admit that she had been just that to him when they'd been growing up.

But she wasn't now.

When he was in the gym lifting weights, his muscles

straining to lift as much as he could, he'd sensed her eyes on him. Her light, distinct perfume had drifted to him, sending warmth through his body.

In the pool while he was taking his morning swim, the chlorine had covered her scent, but when he'd emerged from beneath the water, she'd been there leaning against the wall, pen in hand, scribbling.

*She's just trying to gather useful information, you jerk,* he told himself, but that hadn't helped. Aware that she was watching him as an object to be studied, anger rose within him.

And every time he ran, he was conscious of her, always. The sun was on his back, the wind was in his hair and Eden's gaze followed him. He'd been used to women watching him all his life, but this was different. It was impersonal.

"A good thing," he told himself, except when he glanced over at her as he passed, he'd been aware of the wind in *her* hair. For the first time, without the small details to distract him, he'd noticed the long, graceful curve of her neck, the fact that a man's hand would fit perfectly there in order to pull her closer for a kiss, where perfect vision was unnecessary and only physical sensation mattered.

A curse escaped Jeremy. He had no business thinking of Eden that way. She wasn't here for his pleasure. If he desired her, it was probably because she was the only woman in his life right now. His lust for her was immaterial. She was studying him only to discern how he functioned and what his limits were so she could convey that to the children's parents.

But acknowledging that didn't help his foul mood. No sense sitting here pretending to work when he wasn't getting anything done. He swung away from his desk, put down the magnifier he hadn't been using anyway and strode out of his office into the hallway just as the doorbell rang.

Instantly he realized that Donald was off getting the limo serviced and it was Mrs. Ruskin's day off, so there was no one closer than he was to answer the door. He also became aware of Eden entering the hallway behind him. But she wasn't a servant and she wasn't required to greet visitors. No, Eden was the woman who had been treating him like a lab rat all week. If he asked her to open the door and greet whoever was there she would probably pull out that blasted notebook of hers and...

Jeremy frowned. He moved to the door and opened it. The change from the slight darkness of the house to the brilliance of sunshine worked its ugly magic, as he had grown to expect. His malfunctioning eyes took much longer to adjust than they had in the past. For seconds that felt like minutes, he simply stared at the person on the doorstep, trying to make out...something.

And then old habits kicked in. It was time to be outwardly charming. Anything else might be disastrous. Whoever the person was, he didn't want them to realize he couldn't see, and maybe, despite everything, he didn't want Eden to see him like this yet, either. Telling her about his condition for the sake of the task at hand was one thing. Letting her see the worst of his emasculating weakness was another.

He moved forward, looking toward the unknown visitor. "Hello," he said with a practiced smile. "May I help you?"

For half a second he realized that the person at the door could be carrying a machete or an Uzi and he wouldn't have a clue. Yet, he was chatting amiably to what was, at least temporarily, a total stranger in order to salvage his pride. And from the momentary silence that ensued, he could tell that he must have made some sort of gaffe.

Suddenly the scent of Eden was much closer. "Miriam, how nice. Come on in. You know Jeremy, he always did like to tease. Acting as if he didn't know you…"

Although she wasn't facing him, Jeremy could hear the smile in Eden's voice as she pretended that he had intentionally spoken to Miriam the way he would have to a stranger.

Miriam?

Jeremy wanted to beat his head against the wall as he realized to whom Eden was referring as his vision began to adjust to the light. Ignoring every protesting instinct in his body, he stepped aside to let Miriam DeAngeles in the door. She was no stranger, but not a friend either, despite the fact—or maybe because of the fact—that he and Miriam had been an item for about two months back in high school.

Recently divorced, back in town and looking for a new diversion, she had shown up once or twice lately to borrow a cup of sugar, she had said, although her house was half a mile away. No doubt she read the business section of the paper and knew that Fulton Enterprises was raking in buckets of money. Knowing the woman for what she was and always had been, Donald had made excuses, telling Miriam that Jeremy was working. But that had been last week. Today Donald wasn't here, Eden was unaware of the whole scenario, and…*I can't very well announce to Eden that Miriam is here on a fishing expedition,* Jeremy realized.

This *was* going to be awkward. He was standing here next to Eden, a woman he desired but shouldn't. On his other side was a woman who wanted his lust but in whom he had no interest. Moreover, Miriam could be dangerous when crossed.

She was capable of dropping hints to the media if she discovered what few people knew, that the owner of the Fulton empire was going blind. He would be besieged. And while the truth would, inevitably, be discerned in time…he didn't want to think about that. It was difficult enough living with the unknown and wondering how much of his world would be left when the dust settled. Facing a media onslaught? Being observed like a goldfish in a bowl? Being seen as defective or weak? No.

Yet he was the one who had let Miriam in. Bracing for damage control, he stepped forward.

"Hello, Miriam," he said. "Sorry for putting you on. It's good to see you." Although it wasn't. Miriam was interested in three things only, position, money and gossip, and a better position and more money would always be welcome.

As for gossip? He tried not to visibly react. Miriam was definitely going to wonder what Eden Byars was doing standing beside him welcoming guests almost like a wife.

He waited for the hit, the biting comment.

"Jeremy, hon, I just haven't seen enough of you lately. None, really. That awful man of yours wouldn't let me in. Still, I'm here now and you're looking as edible as ever," Miriam said, stroking a hand down the length of his sleeve, letting her fingers linger just two seconds too long. No mistaking her intent. Miriam was on the prowl. His vision was adjusting to the light, but Jeremy didn't need vision for this.

What's more, he knew what was expected, and giving

Miriam what she wanted was probably the quickest way to deflect her rabid curiosity and get rid of her. "Miriam...thank you. You, of course, are looking beautiful, as always." Which she was, at least on the outside, from what he could see.

Miriam practically purred. She moved closer. And then she turned toward Eden, who was noticeably uncomfortable. Miriam's expression wasn't all that clear from this angle, but he remembered her personality well enough to imagine how she looked. She was wearing the frozen, triumphant smile people wore when they thought they'd defeated a rival. She turned to him.

Ah, confessions were expected. She wanted to know about Eden. The truth about his condition was at stake here, but that wasn't going to happen.

*Skirt the issue, Fulton,* he ordered himself. Not a problem. He had always been a master at throwing up a smoke screen when faced with uncomfortable truths.

"It's good that you stopped by when you did," Jeremy said. "You were just in time to see Eden."

"Oh? Is Eden leaving?" Miriam asked. "I have to say that I'm surprised to find her here, when you've been so distant to your friends lately. Not that I exactly remember you and Eden being close friends when we were younger. In fact, I must be losing my touch, since I seem to have lost track of what Eden has been up to. Maybe that's because she was never a part of my set. You and I ran with a much different crowd. Still, you say she's been... oh...*visiting* you?"

Jeremy felt Eden tense. There had been something nasty in Miriam's voice, as if she thought Eden had dropped by to sleep with Jeremy…for money. For a second he considered ordering Miriam out the door and shutting it in her face. Eden didn't deserve ugly insinuations. But there were more effective ways to deal with nastiness.

"You must have been mistaken about my old friends, Miriam. I hung out with a lot of people you were unaware of, and Eden's family lived right down the block. She's Ash's cousin, you know, and Ashley and I dated a long time." Which wasn't exactly true by normal standards, but by his, three months had been a long time. The fact that his relationship with Ashley had quickly turned from a typical, heated teen event to a platonic friendship wasn't something Miriam would have known. *Platonic* and *friendship* weren't words in her vocabulary. "The Byars are good people," he continued.

And then he heard the most delicious laughter he had ever heard. It wasn't coming from Miriam's direction, either.

Instead, Eden stepped closer to him, close enough that her body was brushing his. She placed a hand on his arm, and heat shot right through him.

"Miriam," she said. "If you want to know something, I'm right here, but…oh my, you didn't really think that Jeremy and I—" She laughed again as if genuinely amused, but her hand trembled where it touched him. "How embarrassing and awkward. The truth about why I'm here is that my cousin Ashley once had a relationship with Jeremy, they're still really good friends and Jeremy mentioned to her that he had a mountain of paperwork and personal correspondence piling up that needed doing this summer, too much for his secretary. Since I was visiting Ashley, and my job teaching school was out for the summer, Ashley asked if I might help out for a few weeks. Why not? Who wouldn't want to help an old friend?

"And see, it's a good thing I did, because now I've gotten to see you, too. It's been a long time, but I remember that you were always laughing."

Miriam had always been laughing at others, Jeremy realized as Eden's grip on his arm tightened. He wasn't sure she even realized that she was touching him.

Turning slightly, he faced Eden, but from the corner of his eye he could see that Miriam's smile was even colder.

"Well, I do try," Miriam said faintly.

"You do," Jeremy said. She tried a lot of things, most of them unsavory. In the past few minutes she had clearly tried to insult Eden. That wasn't going to happen if he could help it.

"Now, is there something Eden and I can do for you, Miriam?" he asked. He covered Eden's hand with his own and felt her jerk, as if she had finally realized that she was touching him, but he gently and firmly held her in place. "Another cup of sugar, perhaps? Yes, Donald did tell me that you've stopped by several times. You must really love to bake."

"Oh. Sugar. Yes. I do love to stir things around," Miriam said, the faintness gone from her voice. "But no, today I was just walking by and thought I'd stop and say hello, be neighborly. And I'm so very glad I did. Otherwise I wouldn't have run into Eden. You make a dutiful little file clerk, dear," she said. "Now, you better get back to sorting those papers. Bye, Jeremy. I'll stop by another time. Not for sugar, though." She stepped back through the door and it clicked closed behind her.

When she had gone, silence set in. Jeremy realized that Eden's hand was still beneath his, warm and soft. "I'm sorry about that," he said, releasing her.

"For holding my hand?"

No, not that, he realized. "For letting Miriam in to try and insult you."

Eden shrugged. "I'm all right."

"It wasn't the first time she did that, was it?"

"The last time I saw her, she was laughing because she recognized the shoes I was wearing were a pair she had disliked and discarded."

Anger slipped through him like a hot knife. "How did you respond to that?"

"I didn't. I never did. I walked away."

Her body was tense. He could feel it. A part of him wanted to move closer and offer comfort, but she wouldn't welcome that. "You didn't walk away today."

And then she laughed again. Softly. So very softly. It was a sound that made a man…want her. Badly. "I didn't, because of the situation. I was playing a part, but I really wanted nothing more than to shut the door in her face."

"I would have loved to have witnessed that." Especially since it mirrored his thoughts.

"Thank goodness I was never very good at following my inclinations," she said. Which made Jeremy raise an eyebrow.

Eden blushed, and he assumed they were both thinking about that long-ago kiss. "Sugar?" she asked, changing the subject.

Jeremy grimaced. "Miriam's husband hunting."

"And you're husband number two?"

"Number three. Or I would be." And wasn't that an uncomfortable subject? Time to change it. "Thank you for stepping in today. I couldn't tell who she was, at first."

"The change in light," she said. She'd obviously done her homework. "Miriam is one of those who doesn't know, does she? If she did...the husband thing?"

"She'd be gone in a flash. Miriam doesn't like weakness."

"I don't think she'd be gone. You're not weak. I've seen you pump iron. And run. And swim." And suddenly the room got very warm. If he'd been wearing a tie, Jeremy would have been tugging on it. He looked down on the top of Eden's head and realized that she had turned away. She was embarrassed at her own comment. And he didn't want her to be. She'd saved his reputation back there. He owed her. A little distraction was in order.

"Believe me, Miriam wouldn't want a man who couldn't see well enough to tell her that her eyes were 'cerulean pools of blue,'" he teased. "She doesn't wear defective goods on her arm, and she'd be climbing over people to get out the door if she knew. Maybe I should just tell her I'm going blind." He grinned. "Maybe you did me a disservice by helping me hide what she would see as my affliction. You may have doomed me. I might have to fork over more cups of sugar."

His teasing had the desired effect. "Maybe she'll ask for a ring and your fortune as well the next time," she said with a smile in her voice.

"In that case," he said, his voice dropping low, "I hope you'll be around to help me run her off again."

Silence followed. She was studying him closely. The tension level had gone up in the room as well as that blasted temperature. "Of course," she said tightly. "I would help.

It's my job. I'm your employee." And with that, she slipped out of the room.

For an entire day she stayed in the library and didn't show up to watch him work out. He should have been pleased. So why wasn't he?

# CHAPTER FIVE

EDEN was back at her post, watching him, and Jeremy was going slowly nuts. He was aware of her physically every minute, especially since that incident with Miriam. He remembered Eden's solemn gray eyes and felt them perusing him. It was almost more than any red-blooded male could reasonably be asked to take, and he had a sudden strong urge to fire Eden, to call Ashley up and tell her it wasn't working.

But that would be a lie.

Eden had thrown herself into the job. She'd been giving him daily progress reports, and it was obvious she'd done her homework. She was growing more knowledgeable about the latest technology and techniques and the most-recent research. One day, when he had been especially busy with a business client, she had even taken a call from Barry, the private investigator, and now the man had taken to asking for her when he called. Jeremy considered the possibility that Eden's professional manner might account for Barry's fascination, but he suspected that the P.I.'s obsession had more to do with Eden's sexy voice and that husky laugh that made a man start wondering where the nearest bed might be.

"If that's the case I'll have to have a talk with him," Jeremy muttered. And tell him what? Not to talk to Eden? As if he had any reason to arrange the woman's life. He didn't, so he wouldn't say anything to Barry. For now. As long as the man treated her with respect and kept his distance....

*Where on earth had she gotten that voice, anyway? Had she always had it?* Jeremy suspected that she had. He just hadn't noticed. But he was darn well noticing now. He increased his pace as he moved into a butterfly stroke and broke the surface, only to find Eden scribbling furiously on her clipboard.

Against his will, something deep and dark ran through him and he knew he should ignore it. It was that deep, dark stuff that had always gotten him into trouble in life. It was that rebellious side that had led him to become a sperm donor...because he'd had an argument with his aunt and he knew she had a thing about not sharing the family genes without her stamp of approval. The woman had raised him out of a sense of duty while despising him every minute. He was too big a reminder of his father, and his father had reminded her of things that *absolutely no one* wanted to remember.

*And I lashed out at her however I could,* he remembered. He had never allowed himself to show his feelings. He'd pretended not to care when she criticized him or compared him to his weak father. But he'd caused trouble wherever he went.

Now, here he was, contemplating trouble again, because heaven knew he shouldn't go near Eden.

"Eden, stop writing," he commanded, resting his arms on the side of the pool.

Startled, she looked up. Was she wearing glasses?

Normally she didn't. But yes, the glasses rested on the end of her nose. They made him notice her narrow, pretty face.

"Why?"

He hesitated, then blew out a frustrated breath. "You've done enough. How much can there be to write about how a man swims?"

For a minute she appeared flustered. He thought she was going to refuse to answer. Without thought, he placed his hands on the side of the pool and in one swift, strong movement swung himself onto the poolside tiles. He strode toward her, water sluicing down his body.

Eden stood up and, thinking he might have frightened her, he stopped. At least his forward movement stopped. In every other way, mind and body, he was racing ahead.

"What *do* you write there?" he asked, motioning toward the paper.

She fidgeted with her shirt, the movement drawing Jeremy's attention down the length of her body to her legs. He stifled a groan. "Do you want me to read it to you?" she asked.

"You don't have to do that, but I'd like you to tell me. You know I can't read it myself without visual aids, so I have to trust you to tell me the truth."

Ah, she raised her chin. He'd made her angry. "I wouldn't lie," she said. "At least not about the important stuff."

He grinned. "I think I know that. What's it say?"

"I don't want to tell you."

Jeremy blinked. "Why not?"

She looked to the side. "There's nothing on the paper."

"Excuse me?" he said, his mind struggling to process that information.

"There's nothing in writing. I've just been watching you."

"I've seen you scribbling."

"I know it looked like that. I guess that was a lie in a way. I was pretending to write."

"Why?" The word came out fast and hard.

"It was…uncomfortable just looking at you and I thought you might be uncomfortable, too, but I really did need to observe you so that I could relay my impressions to the parents."

"Why no writing?"

"Writing is a distraction when you're observing. While I'm writing I might miss something important."

Eden stood there, facing him, clearly uncomfortable— he could swear she was blushing—but not backing away even a little bit. Her courage under such circumstances slayed him.

"So…what *would* you tell the parents?"

She took a deep breath and ducked her head, then she stared straight at him. "I would tell them that the man who fathered their child pushes himself all the time, every day, and he accomplishes a lot. He has bright markers to locate the sides of the pool and while his vision may be weaken- ing, he's still able to make his way around a pool better than most people can. He even dove off the board today…"

Her voice trailed away.

"Yes, that was a stupid thing to do," he said, providing the words she hadn't said.

She tilted her head. "You managed it."

"Barely. I couldn't tell for sure if I was going to walk off the end of the board or not. Only the fact that I've used this board so many times when I was clear-sighted allowed me to do it. I had a good idea of how many steps I needed to take, and when I got to the end I could feel it. You might have noticed that I dove rather wide to make sure I didn't hit my head on a board that was more or less invisible to me."

"I didn't notice. I don't know how to dive. You're talking to a very poor swimmer."

He chuckled. "So…based on what you've observed, would you tell the parents that their children can swim?"

"Of course not! I would tell them that they *might* be able to swim."

"You wouldn't have known that, without all these observations?"

She took a deep breath. "I don't know. It was just… every day you seemed to push yourself more, harder. It seemed as if I needed to know that."

"All right, I can understand that. But I have to tell you, I've pretty much brought out all my swimming tricks." He grinned. "It doesn't get more exciting or eventful than this."

She laughed that pretty, low laugh of hers. "All right. You want me to get lost, don't you?"

*No.* "I just…don't think you need to babysit me anymore."

Now her eyes widened and she took a step forward. "I'm not! I wasn't! Believe me, if you were in trouble swimming, I would be the last person you would want trying to save you. We'd both end up drowning. And you swim better than any normal man I know."

He froze at her words. "Well…that's good to know. I think."

He expected her to apologize, to at least look chagrined, but she didn't do either of those things. Instead she crossed her arms. "Don't you dare get indignant on me, Jeremy. We both know you were *never* a normal man. Not now. Not back when I used to see you in the halls at school."

He raised a brow. "Is that a compliment? Are you trying to tell me that I'm better than normal?" He tried very hard to hide his amusement when she suddenly looked shy.

"Well, I hardly think Miriam DeAngeles would be coming around if she thought you were merely normal," Eden managed to say.

Now, Jeremy couldn't keep from smiling. "I've embarrassed you, haven't I?" he asked.

"I've embarrassed myself, I think," she said, turning toward him, then glancing away.

He reached out and gently tucked one finger beneath her chin so that she was facing him. "Better than normal, Eden? Don't be embarrassed," he whispered. "I've been called a lot of things, some very good, some not so great, some downright terrible, but that's the nicest thing a woman has ever said to me," he told her, and then he dropped what was meant to be a light kiss on her startled lips. Her mouth was soft and warm and pliant and…Jeremy almost groaned as he lifted his head. He turned to go. "No more observations," he told her, his voice rougher than he would have liked. "I'm only a man, and you're an amazingly desirable woman. I don't want to be tempted to kiss you again."

For a minute he could hear her sputtering. "I don't want to kiss you again, either, Jeremy," she said.

He shook his head. "I didn't say I didn't *want* to kiss you. I do…far too much, far too often. Having you here watching me intensifies that desire, but following through and actually touching you isn't smart for either of us. I don't want to get involved with anyone, and neither do you. I don't do family and I don't want children. That's not going to change, so, no more of this. You have all that you need, right?"

She hesitated. "Yes, I've always had all that I need," she finally said, and her tone was so resolute and brave that his heart broke for her. She could say that as often as she wanted. She might even convince herself it was true, but he remembered a very few things about her. One was that she hadn't had what a young girl, any young girl, rich or poor, should have. The temptation to take her in his arms and claim her lips again, completely and thoroughly this time, was almost overpowering.

But he just couldn't do that to her. He didn't trust himself. She deserved so much better than a summer affair, and that was absolutely all he had to offer.

A few days later Jeremy sat behind his desk and tried not to look as if he was staring at Barry Leedman, who was studying Eden with more interest than Eden's question about how much time he spent doing surveillance should have necessitated.

"Sometimes there's not a lot to do except think nice thoughts while I wait," Barry said. "It helps to have something especially nice to think about." Was the man actually leering at Eden? It definitely looked as if he was leaning closer to her.

Jeremy drummed his fingers on the desk. "I think we're ready to get down to business," he said. "Will this take much time? You indicated that a face-to-face interview was necessary. I'm assuming that means you have some important information for me." Or maybe Barry just wanted the chance to stare at Eden's legs, Jeremy thought, noting the way the man's attention seemed to be wandering.

The fact that Barry could actually see Eden's legs better than he could and obviously wouldn't mind running his hands over her naked flesh did nothing to put Jeremy in a better mood. Which was ridiculous. What she and Barry were to each other was none of his business.

Barry had looked up and appeared to be waiting for him. Jeremy realized that *he* was now the one concentrating on Eden. Immediately he sat up and directed his attention to the investigator. "You were saying..." he said to Barry.

The man scrubbed a hand over his face. "I'm afraid I've hit a snag, Mr. Fulton." His voice radiated sincere concern, and immediately Jeremy felt bad for having had negative thoughts about the man. "I thought I was on the trail of a former employee but then that person just disappeared. I suspect he didn't want to talk to me. I also suspect, from my earlier contact with the man, that you *did* actually produce offspring as a result of your contributions to the sperm bank. I believe that there is at least one child, maybe more, but I have no hard evidence. I haven't been able to find out if anyone has suffered any genetic consequences or even managed to locate a child who might benefit from the information or aid you're offering. I'm sorry."

Barry's voice radiated sincerity, and Jeremy remembered that the man was divorced with a son of his own. He'd made no secret of how much the boy meant to him or how much he missed his child. Immediately, any confrontational feelings between the two of them fell away. "It's all right, Barry," he said. "I know you're doing what can be done. We both knew this wouldn't be an easy proposition. People who don't want to be found often can't be found."

"Will you keep looking?" Eden's soft voice slipped into the room.

"Yes," both men said at once.

"Is there anything we can do to help you?" she asked Barry. "That is, I'm sure you're pursuing every lead you have, but maybe we've missed something. There might be questions we haven't asked or a different angle we should approach this from. I guess what I'm saying is that the two of you began this before I ever came on the scene and, admittedly, I don't know much of what you've discussed or of how to conduct an investigation, but…I don't mean to be presumptuous, but you're both…well, men. If we can't locate anyone or any records from the sperm bank…"

When no one responded, her voice trailed off and she frowned. "Of course, I'm sure you have women in your offices who can view things from the perspective of the mothers you're looking for."

Silence followed as Jeremy digested the small but pertinent suggestion she'd just made. He looked up. Was Eden squirming?

"Let's just forget I suggested that," she said suddenly, her voice tentative. "I was just…I don't know. Thinking out loud, I guess."

Jeremy's concentration was on Eden, so he heard rather than saw Barry laugh. "I'm afraid there are no women in my office," Barry said. "It's a small operation, and my assistant is a guy."

*And I would never win any awards for understanding the minds and hearts of women,* Jeremy thought. He'd grown up with a harridan of a woman who couldn't begin to be called either normal or average, he'd dated women without getting to know very much about them, and he hadn't been interviewing his housekeeper or cook to discover their perspectives on the world. And although he could manage that last one, he reasoned, he probably wouldn't, not when right before him there was—

"I'd love to have your help and discuss what the woman or women we're seeking might think," Barry was saying, uttering the words that Jeremy had been thinking. Eden was nodding. The man was opening his mouth again to speak.

"I'll fill you in on my initial discussions with Barry so that you'll know what's already been covered," Jeremy heard himself saying to Eden. "It's all on tape, and I'd like to have your take on things. Anything that would help the case."

"Or help a child," Eden said. Yes, that was what this was all about, wasn't it? Not his bizarre need to try to vie for Eden's attention with a man more whole than himself.

Yet when Barry followed Eden into the library to discuss his part of things, Jeremy had a strong urge to put his fist through a wall.

But that wasn't his way. When facing frustration, speed had always been his style. Fast cars, fast women, fast everything. If a man moved fast enough, his demons couldn't catch him.

Right now he had plenty of demons. A child or maybe multiple children at risk. He closed his eyes and thought about the parents sitting up at night wondering what was going wrong in their child's life and if that child would ever be better. The pain closed in, got in Jeremy's face, attacked.

He tried to turn from it and ran smack up against his

thoughts of Eden, who had grown up differently from those around her. She had been ridiculed and shunned, had had too much responsibility thrust on her and had obviously been hurt by men along the line. She deserved to have a good man like Barry to care for her and mend her. She didn't need someone temporary trying to step between her and Barry.

But the pain spasmed, like a fist clenching around Jeremy's heart. He wanted Eden, and he had the terrible feeling that nothing was going to stop him from taking her and hurting her. It was and always had been his way to grab what he wanted.

*Stop,* he told himself. *Get past it. Do it.*

He rose from his chair. And then he did what he did best. In mere minutes he was outside in the wind and sun. Running. Much faster than was wise.

## CHAPTER SIX

"Thank you for the tea, Mrs. Ruskin," Eden said as the housekeeper set a tray down before her. "You didn't have to do that, but I really appreciate it."

"Lula and I know how to make a person feel at home," the woman said. "We want you to feel welcome here, dear, and it must be difficult holding your own when you have two big men facing off in front of you. Mr. Fulton is...well, he's *ours* and he's wonderful as far as we're concerned, but Mr. Leedman is a hottie, too. And he likes you. I don't think Mr. Fulton is happy about that. He gets that angry caveman look when Mr. Leedman talks to you." The older woman shook her head. "Sometimes, with all that testosterone flowing, a woman needs something soothing. Like tea. You know?"

Eden couldn't help laughing. "I do know," she said as the woman left the room. Although, Eden didn't believe what the housekeeper had tried to imply. Oh, she knew that Barry was interested, and yes, Jeremy had kissed her. Her heart still raced at the memory of his mouth against hers. But that over-too-fast kiss hadn't meant anything. Jeremy was just used to kissing any convenient woman. She had seen that firsthand, and Ashley had talked about the phenomenon enough. If Jeremy was upset, the feeling had more to do with this case than anything.

"Which is good," she told herself. Her goals and Jeremy's were nothing alike. In fact, he wouldn't want to even go near her dream of having children or starting a school. *And* there was one thing more. A big thing.

She and Barry and Lula and Donald and Mrs. Ruskin were all ordinary people. They weren't like Jeremy at all, she thought, staring at the walls that were covered floor to ceiling in leather-bound first editions. Even the air here smelled expensive and rare. Wanting someone like Jeremy to kiss her again was like climbing a cliff when the only way down was to leap off onto the rocks below. Not smart, and—

A shadow flitted past the window, and automatically Eden sat up straighter in her chair. She turned toward the shadow, jumping up from the chair, her heart racing as she looked out the window.

Jeremy had just run past, on the drive this time, not on the grass as he usually did. He was moving fast, really fast and there was something on the ground five feet ahead of him, probably entering his limited field of vision too fast for him to see it.

Pushing at the window and forcing it open, Eden started to yell his name. Too late. He stumbled over the object and went sliding, rolling, ending up hard against a tree.

"Jeremy, no! No, oh no!" she yelled. And then she ran, too, down the stairs and out the door.

The trip down the stairs, through the house and out the door seemed to have taken forever, yet Eden barely remembered it. Her entire focus was on reaching Jeremy, praying that he was all right. She tore across the lawns onto the drive, heading straight for him.

And then she pulled up short. He was sitting on the ground, his strong back against the tree, one knee drawn up in what looked like a casual pose, the other stretched straight out before him. He looked perfectly normal and calm, except his eyes were closed.

"Eden," he said. Just that one word.

Had he been watching? She didn't think so. "Are you all right? I saw—I thought—how could you tell it was me when you don't even have your eyes open?"

The smallest of smiles lifted his lips, and he opened those gorgeous amber eyes. "I can sense you."

She raised one eyebrow. A small startled sound hissed through her lips.

He chuckled. "Don't go all imperious and practical on me. You don't believe me?"

"I…I don't know if I believe you."

And then his laugh deepened. Dark and masculine, the sound curled around her, enticing her to step closer. "Good," he said. "Don't believe everything a man tells you. But I *did* sense you, in a way. I seem to know when you're around and—"

"And what?"

"You smell good. I always know when you enter a room."

His voice was deep and husky. Eden's breathing kicked up. For half a second she remembered his lips on hers, and then she frowned. Something wasn't right here. What wasn't right was that Jeremy had her thinking about kissing him when he had just come up against a tree. "Are you trying to distract me?"

"Why would I do that?"

"I saw you fall. You're hurt, aren't you?"

"Only my pride. I was pushing my limits while letting my mind wander. Not a good combination. Remember that."

"Yes, Mr. Fulton."

He laughed. "Was I lecturing?"

"Yes, but you're allowed. You're my boss." Which was a reminder more to herself than to him. And then, because she couldn't seem to stop herself, she said something more. "You always pushed your limits even when we were young. Why? What drives you to do that when even you just said that it wasn't always smart?"

For a moment she thought he wouldn't answer. "Never mind," she said. "It isn't really my business, is it?"

"I suppose it is when you're the person watching me nearly crash on the rocks. Twice."

She tilted her head. "Twice?"

"The Aston Martin."

"Umm. It *was* a pretty little car."

"There's one just like it in the garage. You can drive it."

Eden nearly choked. "Me? No, I couldn't do that."

He rose to his feet. She saw him wince, but she didn't say a thing. He wouldn't want her to. Then he moved over to her, his body taut in the black running jersey and shorts. Gently he touched her cheek, sending a shiver right through her. "Live a little, Eden. Take some time to play. Drive the Aston if you like. It needs driving, and Donald feels like a hulk in it. It would be a favor to me." Which she suspected was a total lie, so she smiled.

"I might," she promised on a choked whisper.

"I could make it an order," he said.

"But you wouldn't."

He shook his head slowly, his fingers brushing along her jaw. "I wouldn't." He lowered his hand to his side.

"Don't worry, Eden. I push my limits because it feels right. It makes me know that I'm alive, that I'm solid and that I can't be dismissed easily. I suppose my reasons are suspect, however. Growing up, I resented being under my aunt's thumb when she only agreed to raise me out of a sense of family obligation. In fact, she hated me. She'd been in love with my father when they were young, and he had supposedly been in love with her, engaged to her, in fact. But he was a faithless jerk and he got my mother, Aunt Rose's sister, pregnant. And when my parents died young, and I came to live here, Aunt Rose saw him every single time she looked at me. He had been wild, and so was I. The easy thing would have been to let her hatred drive me into hiding, but I didn't. And the easy thing, now that I'm losing my sight, would be to retire into safe pursuits, but I can't, so I push. Amateur therapy, but it works for me."

Eden looked up into his eyes and saw the determination still written there, despite everything. She'd just bet he had never let his aunt see how her cruel attitude had affected him. Instead his pride had kicked in and he had defied the woman. And now he was defying the condition that threatened to rob him of his way of life and dignity.

"If you didn't push, then I guess you wouldn't be who you are," she said softly. "All of that must have helped shape you, and—" she smiled "—Donald tells me that you were practically a genius at Yale, and that other businessmen seek you out because you not only know what you're doing, you have bold ideas you're not afraid to try. And you usually succeed."

"Donald might be a bit biased," he told her with a smile.

"Well, of course he is, but he's also smart and honest. So…don't stop pushing," she said. "I've been reading up. You can still do so much, just differently, perhaps."

He frowned. She knew he didn't want to do things differently.

"All I meant was that you might find a partner when you're out testing fate," she said. "Someone to warn you about obstacles ahead. You already get Donald to play basketball with you."

"That's because Donald likes to play basketball. But at his age and after years of service, he's earned the right to take it easy now and then. I won't make him uncomfortable by asking him to do things he hates just so that I can test my limits."

"So, hire someone else. You have oodles of money."

"Oodles?" he asked with a laugh. "Do people still say oodles?"

"They must. I just did."

"All right, I do have oodles of money. So, you think I should hire someone to be my partner in crime?"

"Why not? I saw you were having a climbing wall built. And there are blind people who bicycle. There are even a few who have taught themselves echolocation and use sounds to locate objects so that they're able to in-line skate and skateboard. I'm not suggesting that, but with a partner…"

"Skateboarding?" he asked. The expression on his face was devious.

"Maybe with a partner," she said, wondering what had

come over her. Why was she acting so bold? She had a terrible feeling that Jeremy's personality was rubbing off on her a bit. She had another terrible feeling that she cared too much about the man, when *he* wasn't why she was here at all. And couldn't ever be. Whether he was a wild and faithless man like his father or not, he was definitely a man who could hurt her badly if she let herself get carried away. And she had already been hurt too much by too many men.

The pain of knowing that her father and uncle hadn't wanted her had taken a long time to get past. She was still bearing the consequences of her mistake of a marriage that had left her alone and in debt. And that had been with a man who had once claimed to care. She had to be more careful around Jeremy.

Searching for common sense and the will to step away, Eden looked down, away from Jeremy's compelling gaze. And then…

She frowned. Staring for a minute, leaning closer, she reached out.

"No. Don't do that." Just before her fingertips met Jeremy's side, he turned away. "You'll get blood on yourself."

"You're hurt," she said. "I didn't even see that before." The irony of that statement, that she, the fully sighted one had missed his injury, came to her, but she didn't care. "We need to take care of this."

"I'm fine. Thank you. I'll think about your suggestion." He turned to go.

Now she knew that he was more badly hurt than he let on. "You don't have to be such an island, you know." She couldn't stop the words.

He whirled back. "Eden?"

She stood her ground. "You know what I mean. When we were growing up you dated all the prettiest girls, but you never let any of them close and you didn't keep any of them. You were an aloof loner who didn't need anyone, and you're obviously still that way. But even if I was mostly invisible to you when we were young, you helped me that day my dog died. You gave me this job when I really needed it and defended me and my family to Miriam. What's more, you're planning to aid those children when you really don't have to, and yet the one time when someone actually has an opportunity to do something for you, when I can give back to you without being paid for the favor, you won't accept it. You have to be invincible." Then, realizing she was lecturing her boss, she froze.

"It was a mistake to say that," she said, horrified. Witnessing his injury and experiencing his touch had wreaked havoc with her emotions and was making her irrational. "I have no right to tell you what to do."

He looked down at her, and she knew he couldn't see her clearly, but it felt as if he saw right through her. He reached out and slid his hand beneath her hair. He drew her close and kissed her. Just once, his lips warm and open over hers so that her head started spinning. *He* had fallen but *she* felt dizzy.

"You *do* have the right to speak your mind, Eden," he said. "I hired you to help me, and you're doing that in more ways than one. The wound is nothing, but I'll get it looked at. And I'll think about what you've said about finding a partner. It might be a challenge finding a man or woman as discreet as you who's also up to the task."

Eden's breath caught for a second. A woman? Well, why not a woman?

There wasn't a single good reason for her to object to that possibility, she admitted, except that the taste of Jeremy was still on her lips and she had spent so much time watching him walk away with other women. She had no right to covet him now. And yet she did.

"So what are you going to do about that?" she asked herself after he had gone.

But she already knew the answer. She was going to follow Jeremy's lead and run. Getting tangled up with Jeremy wasn't an option. She had to keep her distance as much as possible.

Surely that wouldn't be too difficult given the fact that for now her duties were largely confined to doing research. She could easily stay away.

# CHAPTER SEVEN

EDEN was seated beside Jeremy, clipboard in hand, and at his request this time, he acknowledged. She seemed uneasy.

That was probably his fault. He'd kissed her again and made her uncomfortable. That wasn't right. He needed to try to get things back onto a business plane.

"The other day when Barry was here," he said, wading in. "You talked about looking at things from a different perspective and you struck a chord with me." In fact, she'd hit a nerve. All this time he'd been thinking in terms of his own guilt and responsibility, but...

"If you had gone to a sperm bank eight years ago and someone came to you now and you heard that the donor was looking for you, what would you think?" he asked.

He leaned back in his chair, a casual pose, but there was nothing casual about his feelings as he waited for Eden's response. He could sense the intensity swirling through her. But, of course, she had always been serious and intense. Maybe that was part of the reason he'd been reluctant to hire her at first. She felt things so deeply that a man like him could harm her. People *had* hurt her: her uncle, Miriam, her ex-husband, possibly even him. And now? He hadn't been lying before. He had to stop touching her, and yet…

She drew him. He remembered the taste of those warm, wild-berry lips, and every cell in his body ignited and burned. Pleasure and desire coursed through him.

"Eden?" he managed to say, hoping his voice sounded something near normal, not like a man who was lusting after her badly.

"Well," she said, softly. "If I had been in need of a sperm bank, that could mean several things. Maybe I didn't want a man or I couldn't find the right man, but there had probably been some sort of issue with the opposite sex. So, if a man approached me years after the fact and asked me about my child, I'd probably suspect his motives or be frightened, even if he told me there was a medical reason for contacting me."

"So, how would I convince the person that there *is* a real medical reason?"

Eden became even more intense, more still. "You might have to put yourself out there as proof," she said, her voice barely above a whisper.

Jeremy felt himself blanch. That was what he had wanted to avoid all along. To have to be an example, to willingly open up to someone and demonstrate his flaws…he never did that.

"But you might not have to do anything so extreme," Eden said. "Barry told me that he's located a couple of Internet sites where sperm donors and recipients can find each other, if both are willing. He thinks that if I became a presence on them rather than him or you, I might be able to make more headway. With my background as a teacher and the knowledge I've gleaned through research I could at least stress the benefits of contact if anyone knows of any potential candidates. It's a bit of a shot in the dark. The parent would have to either know of the site or know someone who knows of it, but we're going to try."

"You're comfortable doing that?" Jeremy asked. "This wasn't in your job description."

"Well, now that I'm not observing you anymore," she said with a smile, "I'm not sure what to do with all my free time."

He grinned and leaned forward. "Go out and enjoy yourself? Get into the city? Visit a museum? Drive the Aston? Take up skateboarding?" he teased.

She laughed. "I might do some of those things, but I really came here to work."

"You *are* working. You're doing more than I expected. I don't think I'm paying you enough."

A muffled, choked sound slipped from her. "You're talking to a schoolteacher. I'm not used to being well paid."

He thought about that. "And you came here because you needed the work and the money. I'm sure that if I paid you more…"

She crossed her arms beneath her breasts and sat up taller, leaning closer. "I'm not going to lie and say that I don't need the money when you know I do, but—"

"You want children," he reminded her and himself. "You'll need funds." An idea began to form in the back of Jeremy's mind. He rose and circled the desk until he was standing next to Eden.

She raised her chin and looked up at him. Even blurry, she seemed lovely and proud. "No matter what my circumstances are, you're not offering me more money," she said determinedly. And then she rose to face him. She was closer, near enough to touch, near enough to kiss.

Jeremy ordered himself to control his wayward thoughts.

"It could mean that you could have the things you want," he suggested. "The school, the girls you want to help, the babies of your own…"

"Are you trying to seduce me by offering me children?"

Instantly, his world went cold. "You know I'm not."

"I didn't mean it like that. *You* know I didn't. But you're offering me seed money to raise children and to start a school. Money I haven't earned. That feels like seduction."

"You could earn it," he said.

A gasp slipped from her lips. Without even thinking, he leaned forward and placed a hard, quick kiss on that wonderful, plump mouth. She was soft and warm and she swayed toward him. He caught her against him. "Don't think what you're thinking. Despite all the good advice I give myself about being smart and keeping my distance, I love kissing you," he said, "but I would never offer you the indignity of paying you to sleep with me."

"I know that," she said, placing her palms on his chest but not pushing away. "You don't need to pay women to sleep with you. You have to beat them off. Donald tells me that the woman who delivers the groceries has offered herself up if you're interested."

He chuckled. "I'm not." He kissed her again, and the sensation of her soft lips beneath his only made him want her more…which told him he had crossed a line. "I shouldn't keep touching you," he said as he pulled back slightly.

"I know. I like it too much, too."

A groan escaped him. "You've been hurt before, Eden."

"Yes." Now she pushed back.

"Your husband had to have been a jerk. More of a jerk than even I am."

"You're not a jerk."

He smiled. "There are plenty of women who would say otherwise."

He heard rather than saw Eden blow out an impatient breath. "If that's true, and I'm not sure it is, then it's because those women expected something you never promised. You were never permanent. That was always clear, even when we were young, and any woman who gets involved with you has to know that there won't be any promises. She shouldn't have expectations."

"Did you have expectations? Of your husband?"

"Yes. Of course. Because we were married. Promises were made."

"And now you don't want any more promises."

"No. They're too unreliable. Between my father who promised my mother he'd be there and wasn't, my uncle who promised me a home but thought of me as an unwelcome obligation, and my husband who promised me forever but who eventually didn't want me at all, I'm through."

"And you don't want my money even though you could use it."

"Not if I haven't earned it."

"So, we're back to that again. What if you did earn it?"

She leaned back. "Doing what? Is there more that needs doing? Something we haven't thought of? Maybe you do have some of that paperwork we told Miriam about?"

"Sorry, no paperwork, but…someone suggested that I could use a partner…"

"Excuse me?"

He frowned. He knew she wasn't going to like this. He didn't really like it, either, and he didn't want to ask her. Heck, he didn't even want to admit that he really did *have* to ask her, but…

"The other day when I fell…I didn't see that rock in the road. Not even the outline, and…" He turned away. He hated having to say the next part. "I know I really am going to need a partner when I go out because I can't stop testing my limits. I don't want to take on a stranger yet."

He waited, giving her time to digest what he was saying.

"Are you saying— Do you want—"

"I want you. To do all the physical things that I'm doing. To be my eyes in the places where my eyes don't function. Can you do that?"

Seconds of silence followed. "No. I'm sorry. No. Please. I don't think so. I'm…not experienced. I don't do…the things you do. Even with two good eyes, I don't and never did. I wouldn't be good at those kinds of things. I'm not the right person."

He nodded tersely. "All right. I won't push."

"What will you do?"

"I'll find someone." Even though he didn't want to and absolutely hated revealing his weakness to even one more person. "Don't worry. It won't be a problem. Money can buy discretion."

But he could still feel her distress. "Is that all?"

Jeremy shook his head. "We were talking about more work for you, and there's one more possibility, something I've realized I really need. Most of my business I can do from home, and I have capable employees who can handle most of the rest. It's a rare day when I actually have to go out in public, which is good. It means I don't have to pretend or reveal my weakness to the world, but in the next few weeks, I have potential new clients coming to town. A bigger account than usual. The company is wining and dining them, and I'm the face of the company. There'll be social events, and I'll have to be there whether I can find my way around in unfamiliar territory or not. If I have to appear in public, I want to be seen as relatively normal, because in business, power and appearance can be every-thing at times. Eden…"

"Yes," she said immediately. "Yes. That I can do."

Relief and something warmer flowed through him, and yet there was something else, something dark that nudged at him.

"And your reason for agreeing so readily?" he couldn't help asking. She couldn't say money, could she? She'd already turned him down for that. Please don't let it be pity, he thought, even though he was very afraid that it might be pity.

She hesitated. "Will I get to wear a Cinderella dress?" she finally asked.

Jeremy blinked. "The finest."

"Well, then. Why ask? When I was a little girl, I wanted to be Cinderella so badly, but I never got to be the princess, never got to wear the pretty dress or dance with the prince. Opportunities like this just don't fall into the laps of humble schoolteachers. You're asking me to appear in public on the arm of a man women want to kill for and wear a dress that…"

"Women want to kill for," he supplied with a grin.

"Yes. Absolutely."

"And none of this has anything to do with the fact that I played on your emotions?" he asked.

"Of course some of it does. I'm your employee, and I definitely have a personal stake. I know what it is to walk into a crowd and worry about how people will react to me. More than you know. So I really want you to win."

Jeremy couldn't help smiling. "I'll do my best to cross the finish line in the lead." He turned to leave.

"Jeremy, the other stuff. The biking and skateboarding…I'm sorry."

"Not a problem, Eden. It was just a thought," he said as he continued to move. Even though it had been more than that. So far he hadn't let any strangers in on his secret. Everyone who knew of his condition was someone he'd known before and trusted implicitly. The issue could wait a little longer.

Or so he thought.

Later that day, Eden watched Jeremy running across the grass and held her breath as he swung by a tree.

"He knows what he's doing," she assured herself. He did. He was in excellent physical condition. Much more so than she had ever been or ever would be. If it were up to Jeremy, he would be climbing mountains and skiing down hills. He'd probably done both of those things. And she never had.

Why?

Eden took a deep breath. It wasn't something she'd ever lied to herself about. She'd spent her childhood raising her siblings and hadn't had time for physical endeavors. That was partly true. She hadn't had money for skiing or golfing or a lot of other things. That was true, too.

"But even if I had…"

*I hated being conspicuous. I abhorred having people see me mess up.* And she had always felt awkward and clumsy running or jumping or pushing physical limits. She wasn't even remotely good at athletics. She ran funny. She threw funny. Those activities drew attention to her, and she'd spent a lifetime trying to avoid attention. Especially when she was younger. Being the center of attention only reminded everyone of how different she was, of how her clothes were secondhand and ill fitting, of how she was an outsider trespassing in the ranks of the local elite.

That was why she had told Jeremy no.

And that was why he was going to have to look for a stranger to help him expand his physical regimen when she knew darn well that he hated being the center of attention these days.

"So you can continue to be a coward and force the man into doing something he doesn't want to do or…"

Eden stared out the window, waiting. When Jeremy finally appeared in the distance, she studied him. He was tall and broad-shouldered and tempting. And totally off-limits. She had promised herself just last week that she would maintain some distance. But he was paying her well, and she had just discovered this morning that he had increased her wages.

"For the extra work with my business contacts," he'd said.

His actions would clear her debts. They would give her back the piece of her soul that she'd lost in the divorce, and they would enable her to start thinking seriously about her dreams, her school. She would have what she wanted when she left here.

Because he'd taken a chance on her.

She closed her eyes for a while, digesting that. Then swiftly, without allowing herself to think, Eden moved outside. She waited until Jeremy was close.

"Jeremy, can we talk?"

He pulled up short, his muscles tensing, his hair falling over his forehead.

*Temptation.* The word slipped into her consciousness.

"What can I do for you, Eden?" he asked, running one hand over his glistening chest.

*Touch me.* The unexpected thought almost made her gasp. "I was thinking," she said. "About those activities you wanted me to take part in. Bicycling and skating and things like that…"

He shook his head. "I told you not to worry."

"I know, but—"

"Eden," Jeremy drawled with a small smile. "You don't have to be the perpetual good student, always volunteering even when you don't want to."

She frowned. Okay, he was making her angry. "I'm not. I wasn't."

He lifted an eyebrow and she blushed. "Okay, maybe I was, but that's not what I'm doing now."

And now he smiled. "What are you doing now, Eden?"

"I'm…I'm trying something new. I'm being adventurous. If I'm going to run a school I have to be daring now and then."

His incredulous smile grew. "Really?"

She hoped her blush wasn't deepening. "Yes. I think so."

"And what do you propose to do?"

"I'm going to…do what you said. I'm going to be your

partner. I'm going to learn how to do all those things you want to do. Okay?"

"I'm not arguing with you, Eden."

"You're sure I'll do?"

"I'm not looking for a teacher."

"I'm…I really hate looking clumsy and I'll probably be clumsy at most of this stuff."

"Then you won't have to worry. I can't see you all that well."

"All right, then," she said. "Is it agreed?"

"Was there ever a question that I would agree? Where do you want to start? What activity?"

"I…I don't know. I hadn't thought. I thought you would know."

"But you're the one doing me the favor."

"Then, can we start out slowly?"

He tilted his head. "I'll take it as slowly as you like, Eden." And for a moment she thought he was talking about something other than riding a bike.

She nodded. "Good. There's just one thing."

"Tell me."

"I can—I'll *try* to do it all, except…please…not the climbing wall," she said. "I fell from the roof of the house when I was young and—" her voice grew weaker "—I totally panic when I get higher than the first rung on a ladder."

"Then I would never ask that of you," he promised.

She took his hand and put it over her mouth. "I know you can see me some but just in case you can't see how big my smile is, I'm grinning a thank-you for that concession. See?"

Her lips curved upward. He laughed out loud. "No

wall," he said again. "But the other stuff...you might surprise yourself. I'll bet you've never experienced the rush of flying down a hill while the trees zip past."

She hesitated. "Not like you mean, no, but I guess I'm about to have a first time. I hope I don't turn green."

"Me, too," he teased. "And Eden?"

"Yes?"

"Thank you," he said as he turned to leave.

"Jeremy?"

He turned back.

"Have you ever been on a skateboard?" she blurted out. "Or in-line skates?"

A low laugh escaped him. "Not that I can remember. Maybe when I was wild and drank too much in college, but probably not. I played hockey. A lot. And I won't let you get hurt, Eden," he said softly. "In any way. I promise."

"Isn't that supposed to be my job?" she asked.

Slowly he shook his head. "Your job is just to be beside me and to yell at me if I make any false moves. No tough stuff for you. I want your help and I want your company, but I intend for you to be safe. I won't put you in harm's way."

But as she watched him walk away and realized that she had just committed herself to an even closer relationship with him, she knew that she was very much at risk. Jeremy might protect her body, but he couldn't protect her heart.

She was going to have to be smart and do that herself.

"I don't think I'm going to be very good at the skating thing," Eden said a bit breathlessly.

"You'll be fine," Jeremy said with a laugh as he finished lacing up his skates.

"How do you know?"

Jeremy gave her that trust-me-sweetheart look that had slain better women than she was. "I mentioned that I used to play a lot of hockey. Despite the difference between metal blades and wheels, much of the concept is the same. Now, let's make sure you're ready."

He gave her that slightly sideways look that she was beginning to get used to. Heck, she was even beginning to think of it as sexy, since it always meant that he was studying her. Except it also made her heartbeat speed up, and her breathing and…

"Why are you frowning at me?" she asked.

"You're not wearing knee pads."

"Neither are you."

"Yes, but I like to live dangerously. You don't," he said. "And I don't want you getting hurt on my watch."

Eden opened her mouth to protest. And then she closed it. Jeremy already lived with enough guilt, and he had a strong need to push back at fate. She put on the knee pads. "Show me what to do," she said.

"Push off like this," he told her, demonstrating. She tried a few tentative steps, her movements jerky and slow.

"Not bad," he said.

"You're just saying that because you can't see how awful I am or that my eyes are rolling back in my head."

He froze. "I'm sorry," she said.

"I'm not," he said with a smile. "I love that you do that, that you feel comfortable enough to tease me about it."

"I didn't mean to be insensitive. I was just so nervous and afraid of falling that I struck out in a very bad way."

He skated close and cupped his hands beneath her

elbows. "Shh," he said. "Don't do that. Don't be careful with me. Just be natural. If you need to strike out, do it. I can take it. I don't want to be coddled or treated differently. All right?"

She nodded. "Yes." His hands were rubbing slow, gentle circles on her skin. Her heart was slamming around inside her chest. "Yes. All right."

"Were your eyes really rolling back in your head?"

"A little. No, a lot."

"That's a shame. We really need one good pair of eyes between us."

She smiled and leaned forward, her mouth almost touching him. "All right. I'll be the eyes. You be the skill."

"That sounds like a great plan." He backed away, and then he reached out and took her by the hand. "Let's let the wind blow through our hair, Cinderella. Lead on."

"We might wobble a bit at first."

"Wobbling works. It leads to other things. Sliding. Racing."

"Never."

But before she knew it, with Jeremy's hand holding hers tightly, Eden was moving around the circular drive. When she slipped, he held on and lifted her. Sometimes he slowed them down until she found her bearings but then they were off again.

"A pebble straight ahead," she said, and Jeremy swung them wide.

"We're at the turn," she directed and he showed her how to crossover her skates so that they went around the bend relatively smoothly.

"This is amazing!" she said, even though her ankles

bent in ways that ankles were never meant to bend and she was moving at turtle speed half the time and still wobbling a lot. "I can't believe we're doing this. I can't believe *I'm* doing it. I've always had two left feet."

"No, not true. You just didn't have opportunities to practice. You had to get your bearings. We'll have to try a rink someday," he said in that low, seductive voice that caught her off guard and kept her breathless all the time.

"A rink? Why would we want to do that?"

"Music," he whispered. "And dancing, Cinderella. You can even wear one of those frothy skirts that flow out behind you and be Cinderella on blades."

It sounded wonderful. But later, when Mrs. Ruskin called Jeremy in to take a business call, Eden had time to think, and she knew that the Cinderella part wouldn't happen. This was only a very temporary position. Once they located any children and made contact, she would be gone, back to the only life she could really trust, one where she was alone and running the show, reliant on no one but herself. And Jeremy would be on to his next female companion. *She* might be in the picture now, but once he had gotten past this mission, he would get back to the rest of his life, and there would always be women in Jeremy's life.

And those women wouldn't be employees pretending to be fairy-tale goddesses. They'd be the real deal. Born-to-this-world rich princesses who fit into Jeremy's lifestyle perfectly. *Remember that. Don't daydream about him anymore,* she thought.

That was excellent advice. Someone ought to take it.

# CHAPTER EIGHT

"MS. BYARS, it's very nice to meet you." Jonathan DeFray, CEO of the company whose account Jeremy was trying to win, took Eden's hand in his own. "Mr. Fulton tells me that you're an invaluable assistant."

She smiled despite a bad case of nerves. Her duties today were simple, but Jonathan DeFray was one of those businessmen so successful that he was a local household name. This was a major account, and every second today mattered. "Well, Mr. Fulton is very easy to work for," she said. "He knows exactly what he wants and that always makes his employees' jobs easier."

The man laughed even though Eden knew she hadn't said anything funny. "A perfect answer, Ms. Byars. Talk up your employer. Be loyal. I like that."

He made it sound as if she were acting, but she wasn't.

"Okay, Fulton, let's get down to business," the man said. "Show me what you have for me. And by the way, thank you for inviting me to your house. This is pretty darn impressive, even for the rich and famous."

"What can I say? The Fulton forefathers liked things big and showy," Jeremy said, in that casual, teasing way he had.

The man laughed. "So do I."

"Well then, let's see if I can follow through on that premise today. Shall we get started?"

"Can't wait to see what you have for me."

Jeremy nodded. "Eden?"

She knew what to do. "Mr. DeFray, please sit here so you can see better," she told him, seating him in a chair that had been placed to give Jeremy a relatively good view of the man. There was a monitor hanging on the wall that Jeremy faced. It was attached to a laptop, and he held a pointer. Eden knew that while Jeremy was perfectly capable of carrying out his business with visual aids, he didn't want to use them today and when he faced the screen head-on he couldn't see the complete details of what was there. He also couldn't see all the details of the man he was trying to sell to.

But he had trained himself well. He'd memorized the placement of what was on each slide. Now as he moved through his presentation, he pointed out details perfectly. "I've done an assessment of your company, Jon, and frankly, for the moment your system is sufficient for what you need it to do. The question is what you'll want it to do two years from now, five years from now and beyond."

Eden looked at Jonathan DeFray and saw the surprise in his eyes. "You're telling me that if I said I wanted to hire your company but not expand, I could sit tight and you'd be totally fine with that? In spite of the fact that we both know I can afford to buy anything I want to?" His hands tensed ever so slightly on the pencil he was holding. This was obviously an important question.

"You could pretty much do nothing and you'd still be

fine. Other than the usual minor updates of systems to keep up with current technology you could make only minimal changes in the short-term," Jeremy said.

"Oh yes, always those minimal changes."

"I'm not going to lie to you, yes. The world of computers always involves change."

"Hah!" the man said with a laugh. "I like your attitude. It shows strength of character that you didn't try to tell me I could get by with absolutely no outlay of cash at all. Lots of people would do that and then they'd sell me a bill of goods. Are you going to sell me something else?"

Jeremy grinned. "I don't know. Am I? I'd say that depends on what you want. You can stay put and we'll make sure that you don't fall behind, keeping you up to date on the current technology with a minimal outlay on your part, or if you want to dress things up and add some sparklers or some heavy-duty fireworks to light things up and go for the big, showy, impressive display, we can do that, as well. Your call."

Eden looked toward the client. He looked as enchanted as any woman who had ever set her sights on Jeremy. His mouth was open, and he was leaning forward. Then, he turned and winked at Eden. "Fireworks? Your boss has obviously done his homework. It's a bit of a secret that I'm into amateur pyrotechnics. And it's always good to do business with people who are thorough, know exactly who they're dealing with and don't just sit back and wait for things to happen. Your boss is a bit of a legend in the business," Jonathan DeFray told her. "Because he knows which buttons to press and how to seduce clients over to his side. All right," he said to Jeremy. "Now that I know a bit more about how you operate, let's get down to the basics. Let me tell you what I really want and you tell me whether you think it's doable." He began to spill out his wish list.

Eden took a deep, silent breath and glanced at Jeremy who looked completely casual and at ease despite the fact that she knew he didn't want Jonathan DeFray to know that he was dealing with a man whose eyesight had moved beyond merely failing to on-the-road-to-being-legally-blind. This was where she came in. Jeremy repeated the names of the catalogs that would most likely contain the products that would fulfill the wish list. Eden stepped to the table in the corner where Jeremy had everything organized. She pulled out the huge tomes and carried them over to a table Jeremy had invited DeFray to move to. She did her best to merely look like a minion doing the grunt work, when in fact her duty was to make sure Jeremy had the right book without having to fumble through the stack.

"The Scarsdale collection," she said, placing one of the tomes in the center of the table.

Jeremy didn't blink. "I think you'll find the large-scale wall-mount monitors on page 211 might meet your needs, DeFray," he said. "Let me show you."

Eden opened the book to the place Jeremy had indicated. "The Fulton 3000?" she asked, indicating that she had the page on display.

"Exactly. Look at this, DeFray. What do you think?" Jeremy reached out and ran a hand over the page, stopping at one of the models illustrated there. His movement was more of a careful measured slide down the page than anything, and Eden wondered if Jonathan DeFray noticed that Jeremy was using a hand span to figure out how far down the page the item was, but the client was simply staring at the monitor Jeremy was indicating.

"If you're looking for a full-scale computerized operation and you have the room for something this size, this could be what you want," Jeremy told him. "With these and the necessary cams, networking between offices or even between the cafeteria and an office would be possible at the drop of a hat. These are large enough that no one in the room will have to strain to see what's going on. They're big enough to have impressive demos when you have visiting clients, and if you really want to go all out, I have a gallery I work with that creates framed work to place over these so that your offices have more ambiance if the screens aren't needed for a while."

The two men began to discuss the pros and cons of various systems. Jeremy always mentioned the name of the catalog and the page the item in mind was located on so that all Eden had to do was move things around and locate the pages.

Within a short time the table was littered with catalogs, and Jonathan had made some preliminary decisions. He had rolled his chair over to the display table and now left it to look at a mock-up Jeremy had called up on a computer screen, complete with the products the man had selected. When Jeremy began to follow him, the wheel on the chair protruded slightly and was directly in his path. Eden automatically reached out and placed her hand on Jeremy's arm.

The slight movement caught Jonathan's attention, and she could feel herself blushing. "I'm sorry, I didn't mean to step in your way," she said, acting as if she had touched Jeremy's arm in order to catch herself. "I'll just put these catalogs away." She slid the chair out of Jeremy's path, making as much noise as was possible with a well-oiled chair.

Jonathan chuckled. "Fulton, if I didn't know better, I'd say that your Ms. Byars was interested in you," he said. "Especially the way she's blushing. I love a woman who blushes. It's positively erotic."

Eden had her back to the men now and she expected Jeremy to react with his usual, laid-back, casual humor. Instead the room was silent. She turned around.

"I hope you didn't mean that the way it sounded, DeFray," Jeremy said. "Because Eden is entirely professional. She's here to help make this meeting flow more smoothly and she's done so. She deserves our respect. I'm afraid I don't take kindly to people making insinuations about my employees."

Suddenly the room was supercharged. What on earth was Jeremy doing, Eden thought. He'd spent days, maybe weeks preparing for this meeting. He had used all the skills he possessed to present himself as a strong, in-charge, no-flaws businessman, and Jonathan DeFray was on the verge of emptying multiple treasure chests to buy the equipment and expertise of Fulton Enterprises. But all of that could end right here and now if DeFray took offense.

"Eden is my employee and yes, she's also a friend," Jeremy continued. "In fact, I've known her since we were children. I won't sacrifice that kind of genuine friendship for business, ever. A man needs to know what is important in life. This woman is more important than an impressive new account."

For a minute the room felt frozen. The men faced each other. Jeremy seemed to be staring directly at the man, his face an unforgiving mask.

Then the other man smiled. "My apologies. You're right

that I was out of line, Fulton. I spoke without thinking and there's no excuse for that. Furthermore, I like a man who knows what matters and doesn't back down. Ms. Byars, forgive me if I offended you in any way," he said turning to her. "I need to watch my thoughts and my mouth at times."

"No offense taken," she said mildly, returning to her work. Her entire body was on alert. Her hands were unsteady. Jeremy had risked a major account just because the client had said something mildly suggestive about her, and she needed time to put that in perspective. She needed not to let herself make too much of that or be too affected by it. It was just Jeremy's way, like the event with her dog. He had been treated unjustly by his aunt and so he was a strong believer in justice. That was all it was, and she had to let it pass and not let her heart melt over the incident.

"Let's write the whole darn package up, Fulton. Get Ms. Byars to do the honors and set the wheels in motion."

Now she was outside her sphere. Jeremy did have a wonderful secretary, but Arrabelle Quinn couldn't seem to manage a meeting like this without staring at Jeremy constantly or trying to help him around the room. It bothered Arrabelle terribly to see him fading this way, so she was waiting for the paperwork to be handed to her, when she would then work her own miracle completing a stunning presentation package. Then DeFray could go back and show his people all the pretty new toys he had bought and what he was spending and how this was going to make them all happy and make their jobs easier. In her own way, Arrabelle was a sales team of her own.

Still, the woman couldn't be here now, so Eden sat down and scribbled the basics on paper. "This will be typed up and sent off as soon as possible," she assured DeFray. "Mr. Fulton has a full staff to handle it."

Which seemed to make the man very happy. "Good. Every successful businessman needs to have lots of strong and talented worker bees." Then the man sighed. He ran a hand through his hair. "You know, for all the money and power I have and despite the fact that I know computers are a necessity, I hate buying the darn things. Talking about them makes me nuts. Having to spend money on them makes me even crazier, and I really wasn't looking forward to this meeting. You made it easy, though, Fulton, and pretty painless. Come on, let me take you to lunch to celebrate the fact that we've come to terms. My secretary gave me the name of a great restaurant in the city."

Eden wanted to groan. With success so close at hand, Jeremy wouldn't want to take a chance on going out in public where he wouldn't automatically know the lay of the land and might chance appearing weak in his new client's eyes.

She cleared her throat tentatively. "Mr. DeFray, that's an excellent idea," she said, "except I know that Lula, Mr. Fulton's cook, is really hoping you'll stay to lunch here." Where Jeremy would be in his own safe territory, where he could negotiate with ease.

She looked up to meet Jeremy's grin. Lula had not been informed of any guests for lunch, she knew.

"That's wonderful, Eden," Jeremy said. "Lula's cooking is the stuff a man would kill for, DeFray. It's not to be missed. Eden, maybe you should go see Lula and check on when we might expect to eat. Let her know that we're done here. She'll be thrilled at the chance to show off her skills to Jonathan, especially if she's been slaving away all morning in order to make him something impressive."

Eden wanted to scowl at Jeremy for teasing her, but she gave him a sweet smile and made a humming sound that would let him know she was on to him even if he didn't catch her mocking expression. The darn man knew that as soon as she cleared the door, she would have to sprint to the kitchen and pray that Lula could come through for her. She hoped that she hadn't messed up too badly this time.

The meal had been a good idea, Jeremy had to concede two hours later when DeFray finally left, although he was afraid it had put too much of a strain on Eden. Not knowing her, DeFray wouldn't have noticed her stress, but Jeremy had been aware of it the entire morning.

He came up behind her after DeFray had rolled off in his Jaguar. "You were pretty magnificent today. Thank you for your help."

"I didn't do all that much."

"You made sure I didn't fall over anything, and you made sure I didn't look weak. DeFray is a decent guy in his way, but he's also the sort who senses cracks in a person's veneer and considers them a weakness. Although he must have some disabled people among his rank and file employees, he doesn't have to interact with them one-on-one, so he doesn't have to reveal his discomfort. With this new relationship, he and I will have several prominent meetings. He'll want to appear confident and proud of our new relationship in front of his partners and business associates, not awkward. We wouldn't have landed this account if the truth had been known."

"That's offensive."

"In his case, I don't think it's an intentional or even a conscious thing. He'd probably be surprised and offended himself if it was brought to his attention, but he still would feel awkward in my presence if he knew the truth."

She frowned. "Then you shouldn't let him have your business."

Jeremy laughed. "If I did a scan of every client and eliminated those who have opinions I don't agree with, I wouldn't have any business. You probably wouldn't have any students or at least you wouldn't if you decided their parents had to conform to a standard of behavior. People sometimes have biases, Eden."

"I know that. I don't have to like it."

He smiled. "And I'm sure you try to change their opinions."

"Yes," she said primly.

"Then you're the secret to the world improving. People like you, and teachers like you, make the world turn and change. And you did help me today. A great deal of my business is handled by my employees and salespeople. I don't get involved unless, in prominent cases such as this one, the client insists on dealing with me personally. I've been able to avoid these kinds of situations for the most part, but today I couldn't. That might have been problematic, and you know I'm not—I can't go public with my situation. When it happens, I want to choose the time and do it my way, not have it happen accidentally. So, I needed you today. I didn't worry with you there. I could concentrate on the things I know best and ignore my concerns that I would slip up. Thank you."

She sighed. "You're welcome."

"Although moving our guest's glass away from the edge of the table did go above and beyond the call of duty, I think." Jeremy smiled. He saw Eden jerk slightly.

A frustrated sigh slid from that pretty mouth. "Don't remind me. I can't believe I actually did that. It's a teacher thing and maybe a mom thing from all the years of raising my siblings. I wasn't even aware…I just did it. Do you think he was offended?"

"I think he was enchanted that you cared. You do have a lot of parenting experience, don't you? All those siblings?"

She shrugged. "My mother wasn't really available to do the job." She took a deep breath. "She was an alcoholic. I don't think I've ever mentioned that. To anyone, not even to Ashley, although, she knew, of course."

"Eden…" he said, and without thought he drew her into his arms. "I didn't know. Of course I didn't. Ashley wouldn't have shared that. Your childhood must have been difficult."

She rested there against his heart, feeling as if she had been made to be there. "I did love her. It was a sickness she couldn't seem to help made worse when my father left us, and I had the girls to raise. I love them to death, so it wasn't totally awful. Some of it was pretty wonderful in ways." She was talking fast. Too fast. He was sure that everything she said was true, but he knew her life could not have been easy.

"Today must have been a bit of a flashback. Having someone lean and rely on you to cover for any mistakes made."

Immediately she pulled back. "No! Don't think that. It

wasn't at all like that. I—you're so obviously a master at what you do. I've heard all the stories about how your employees love you and your clients revere what you do. I was just there today as a helper for the show. I didn't feel as if the weight of the whole show was on my shoulders."

He cupped his hands around her face. "I would never ask that of you. I don't want to ask more of you than you feel comfortable giving, so…tell me if I ever cross the line."

His lips were a mere breath from hers, and he knew he was very much in danger of crossing the line right now. Her mouth was pure temptation, the scent of her drew him, enticed him. Her body felt so right this close. He wanted her closer.

"Tell me," he said again.

"I will," she said, the words coming out on a soft breath. "I promise I will."

The phone rang, and the sound seemed to break the spell. Jeremy nearly groaned, but immediately he released Eden and tried to forget that he had been on the verge of pulling her closer, tasting her, taking it further and touching her in ways that would have been difficult to explain or call back. Several seconds later, the intercom buzzed.

"Mr. Fulton, that's Mr. Leedman on the line. He wants to come over right now. He says he has something important to report to you."

In that instant the world turned dark. The truth marched into Jeremy's life with a horrible, dissonant clatter. There must be a child, someone he had potentially harmed, someone whose life might be changed forever because of him, and not in a good way.

"Tell him to come," he told Mrs. Ruskin as he looked at Eden.

"Do you want me to stay or go so that you can talk to Barry in private?" Eden asked.

Jeremy's reaction was immediate and powerful. *Stay*, he thought. He wanted her with him…too much and for more reasons than he cared to examine. That fact sent up red flags and told him to back off. Being the support system for others might have been the pattern of her life, but he didn't want to blithely join the herd of people taking what she offered, then turning away. Most of all he didn't want to start missing her when she wasn't around.

But this meeting was at the heart of why he'd hired her. This was just a service he was paying her for.

"Stay." He finally said the word. Now that he had acknowledged the danger, he could control the outcome.

# CHAPTER NINE

"THERE'S definitely a child," Barry had said. Eden remembered the moment so clearly. "One child."

The words had fallen into the room like a bomb exploding, tearing things apart and then leaving a terrible silence in its wake.

Her glance had immediately gone to Jeremy, who was white-lipped, the muscles in his jaw taut. "You're sure? How do you know?"

Barry shook his head. "The first employee I talked to disappeared, but he had spoken to some of his former colleagues and there was one woman who remembered you quite well. She felt that you should know the truth."

"It was so long ago," Eden had said. "How could she be sure?"

Barry looked uncomfortable. "Each donor at the registry was given a code to identify him. Jeremy was...let's just say you impressed the staff," Barry told Jeremy.

In other instances, this would have been a light moment, Eden thought. There was no question what Barry was referring to. Jeremy had been an impressive specimen of a man even in his younger years. Not as much as he was now, she admitted, staring at the man who crept into her most innocent dreams and turned the heat factor up many degrees. But he had always been memorable. She understood exactly what the woman had meant.

"The staff apparently spoke freely about Donor 465 and about the lucky woman whose children would receive his DNA. This particular employee admitted she had been smitten. Donor 465 had seemed more mysterious than most, more evasive, attractive and temporary. Because he quit the program earlier than usual, the odds of positive results weren't that great. So, when it became known that there had, in fact, been a positive result, she had noted it. The staff had discussed it. There's no question in her mind that there was a child and only one child. Unfortunately, that's all she knows. However, the identification code is key."

"I hadn't even paid any attention to it," Jeremy admitted. "I didn't take note of it. That was how careless my decision to donate had been."

His voice was grim, and Barry left soon afterward with Jeremy's thanks and with Barry's promise to keep pursuing a lead to the child in question.

After he had gone, the room went silent.

"A child, Eden. An innocent human being," Jeremy said.

Eden didn't bother saying that at least there was only one. She knew better than anyone that every child counted. So, apparently, did Jeremy. But she couldn't leave him with this gut-wrenching guilt.

"You know the odds. There's a definite chance that there won't be a problem," she said.

Jeremy turned toward her. The smallest of smiles lifted his lips.

"I'll bet you brought happiness to your sisters' lives, despite what they had to deal with every day. You must be a heck of a good teacher. Ashley was right about you, you know."

In a different situation that comment might have made her day, but not today. Jeremy was bearing a heavy weight, traveling a path where she couldn't follow, Eden thought as she left him.

"How can I help?" she asked her silent room.

No answers came. She was, after all, just an employee hired to do a job, and her task today had been completed. Trying to do more wouldn't be welcome or smart.

"So when have you ever been smart where Jeremy is concerned?" she whispered as she began to make plans.

Jeremy sat at his desk and tried to empty his mind, but it was impossible.

*The child was real. Somewhere his defective DNA lived in another human being and changed that person's life.*

A definite chance there would be no problem, Eden had said. Jeremy's throat hurt at the sweetness of that statement. She was trying so hard to help him. What had he ever done to deserve that kind of genuine goodness?

"Not a damn thing." And too many things all his life that proved he didn't deserve to have Eden on his side. He'd dated girls and then left them once he realized that his aunt approved of them. He'd wrecked more cars than he could remember. He'd flaunted all the rules at home and at school. He'd helped conceive a child every bit as carelessly as his poor-excuse-for-a-human-being father. None of that could be relived. Now a child or that child's children might suffer the results of his rash actions. And Eden was worried and hurting for him. He hated that he was doing that to her.

If there was justice in the world, he supposed his aunt was somewhere whooping it up and regaling herself with the knowledge that he was finally paying for his sins. Blindness had stopped him in his tracks. It made it impossible for him to come to a woman whole. The future was unclear in more ways than one, and he had nothing to offer.

Jeremy wanted to yell. Instead, with the last light of day, he forced himself to do what he hadn't done since Eden's arrival. He stared straight ahead and took stock. The dark areas of his visual field were larger than they had been. He knew there was a clock directly in front of him, but he couldn't see enough of it to tell the time. Carefully, he mentally measured what he *could* see, the area of the periphery that was still distinct.

Smaller. A touch smaller than before.

His heart squeezed. He battled the loneliness of his condition and came up swinging.

"Fight, Fulton," he ordered himself. "Keep going."

All right. But what could he tell the child? And what would he do when it was time to let Eden go? That time was coming up fast. Summer was slipping away, and a darkness unrelated to his blindness gripped him. He was starting to have feelings for her that couldn't be acted on.

Which meant that he needed to take a step back from Eden.

It was so easy to want to do something and so difficult to actually do anything that mattered, Eden realized a few days later. The pipeline of information had stopped. Barry had nothing more to give them. Eden had no solutions. And Jeremy had been distant, cool, formal and mostly absent.

She knew why. Jeremy had spent his life as a rebel. Stung by his aunt's hatred, he had hit back and had unintentionally harmed a child. In his eyes, he was now every bit as selfish as his father and as cruel as his aunt.

Eden's heart hurt at the thought. She wanted Jeremy to revert to the laughing, carefree man who made women fall in love with him just by breathing. She missed him, but what could she do?

*Find the child.* If his recipient child was found and turned out to be free from any genetic markers of the disease, that would help a lot.

And if the opposite was true? If the child had inherited Jeremy's condition?

Eden closed her eyes and turned to her computer. There had to be other avenues to learn the truth, stones left unturned. She picked up her phone and called Barry.

"There *are* avenues, but none of them are perfect or particularly reliable," he told her, naming some of the steps he was taking. She wrote down Internet links and sites.

"Barry?" she said.

"Yes?"

"I didn't tell Jeremy I was calling. Just so you know." She didn't ask him not to tell, although she hoped he wouldn't. It felt wrong to be following paths backward and delving into Jeremy's past without his knowledge, but she couldn't not try.

"All right. I know now," Barry said with a sigh.

"Thank you."

"Just be careful, Eden. Jeremy's not an easy man to get close to. He may seem dazzling but if you fall in love with him you might get hurt."

As if she hadn't known that. "That won't be a problem. I'm too smart to take risks," she promised, hoping that it was true.

The day dragged on. She went to lunch and ate alone. She went to dinner and ate alone. She stayed up all night at her computer screen. When the morning came she knew nothing more than she had known the day before.

And still Jeremy didn't put in an appearance. According to Mrs. Ruskin he was working in his offices. Most likely he was, given the fact that he had a new client who would be expecting results, and yet they had not discussed the child and...

He's cut himself off from the world, and there's nothing to tempt him to come out, Eden thought, staring out the window to where the gardener was trimming the lawn around the yet-to-be-used climbing wall.

A glimmer of an idea lit in her. Jeremy might beat up on himself twenty-four hours a day, but he had a protective streak for those in his care. Of course, doing what she was thinking of doing would be totally out of character. It would mean overcoming fears she didn't want to think about. Nausea began to chase her down and attack.

"Ignore it," she told herself. "Don't think. Just do."

Immediately, Eden stood up and rushed to her room. The words *Don't think, don't think, don't think* ran through her mind as she threw on jeans and a white T-shirt and hurried down the stairs.

"Donald," she called when she saw him. "Do you know

how to use that contraption?" She pointed toward the wall that was visible from every window on the south side of the house.

"I've done some climbing, and Mr. Fulton had some trainers teach me what I needed to know."

"Good, because I don't have a clue. I just know I'm going up. Not too high, though."

"Are you sure about this?"

She was sure she was crazy to be doing something that frightened her so much, especially when she wasn't even remotely certain that her plan would work. Already dizziness was threatening. It was all she could do to keep herself from turning around and running back to her room. Somehow, she managed to stay put. "They even have climbing walls at schools now, Donald," she said, trying to seem nonchalant. "Maybe I'll be able to make use of this somewhere else someday."

"Okay, but you're right that you're not going up too high," Donald warned her. "I like you, and Mr. Fulton has given you free rein, but I don't like the fact that we're doing this without his knowledge."

"He's not available, Donald."

"I know that," he grumbled, looking almost as unhappy as Eden felt as he showed her how to put on the harness and got her set up.

Eden looked up the wall. It wasn't terribly high, she supposed, but for a woman who experienced mind-numbing terror on a step ladder, the massive surface seemed threatening.

Still, she put on her helmet, tested the feel of the harness and reached out for the first handhold. It felt very small, too inconsequential, but she placed her foot on the next foothold and drew herself up. She was officially off the ground. And feeling about as awkward and frightened as she could remember. Her stomach clenched, her head spun. *Get down, go back,* her brain ordered.

"How's that?" she asked Donald, her voice shaking.

This time he smiled. She must be all of one foot off the ground. "You're doing just fine, Eden. I don't know why you're doing this, but…are you done yet?"

*Yes,* her cowardly brain commanded. But she hadn't achieved her goal yet. She looked toward the window where Jeremy's office was situated, then quickly looked away. Thinking of him would only make her more nervous and frightened.

She reached for another handhold. Another. *Deep breaths. Deep breaths. Don't freeze. Don't get sick.* Her head was swimming, but still she kept going. She clutched at the next handhold, her stomach lurching, her mind panicking.

"Donald?" she asked, her breath completely shaky and shallow now. "How am I doing, do you think?"

"You're doing absolutely perfect for a woman who's deathly afraid of heights." Jeremy's cool, deep voice sounded below her and for a second Eden shrieked and lost her grip. She dangled in the air, Jeremy holding the belay line firmly as nausea slapped at her.

She looked down at the ground, which seemed incredibly far away. In truth it was only about a dozen feet but…

"I didn't mean to go this far. What was I thinking?" she said.

She expected him to laugh. Lots of people would have. There was probably no reason at all to be frightened. But Jeremy wasn't laughing. "I have you, Eden, and I would never let you fall. Just slowly reach out in front of you and grasp the next handhold. Don't look down. Look at your hands. Look at the rock."

That was the last thing she wanted to do. She wanted to go down, not up. But she was the one who had started this whole thing, and she had had a darn good reason, too.

"Do you hear me, Eden? Grasp the rock."

"Can you see it?" she asked.

"No, it's a blur, but I know it's there, and I can see enough to manage my part. You need to find a handhold and a foothold. Grasp the rock. Do it."

"Yes." His voice compelled her as it always did. She took the next step and did as he said.

"Now another step up."

She did it. A sense of exultation began to come over her. Jeremy was holding the rope, giving her slack when she needed it, but exerting control the whole time. He wouldn't let her fall.

"One more," she said, and she thought she heard him laugh, but he gave her enough slack to ascend one more step.

"I'm there. I'm up," she said exultantly.

"Fantastic," he said. "Now, let's get you down from there."

Within moments she was back almost on the ground. Jeremy caught her in his strong arms the minute her toe touched the grass and he turned her around to face him. "Imagine my surprise when through my window I heard you tell Don you were going up. Feel a strong urge to leave the ground today?" he asked.

Eden felt her face flame. He knew it wasn't true. She raised her chin. "I felt a strong urge to see my boss's face. I was out of work."

"Ah," he said with that smile she had missed. "I guess I'd better find more things to do to keep you from risking your neck."

"Donald has had training," she explained.

"But you haven't and you don't like heights. When people are afraid they sometimes do foolish things."

Oh, didn't she just know all about that? "I was perfectly safe, I'm sure."

He smiled but it was a sad smile. "Tell me again why you did this when it was so obviously not on your list of things to do in this lifetime?"

She crossed her arms and leaned closer. "You disappeared. I didn't think that was healthy."

"How did you know I would come?"

"It's who you are."

He opened his mouth. To protest, Eden guessed, so she shook her head vehemently, so that the gesture couldn't be missed. "I hoped you would show up, and you did."

"Because you needed work?"

"And...the other."

"Oh, yes, you think I'm not taking care of myself." Jeremy's voice was a low caress. He reached out and gently brushed his knuckles across her cheek. Then he took off her helmet, her dark hair falling free. "You did this because you wanted to help me, but I'm not one of your students, Eden."

Eden looked up, straight into Jeremy's eyes. He was so close, so warm. "I know that," she somehow managed to say. "But after you heard about the child..."

He waited, leaned closer, much closer. She felt his hands in her hair.

She closed her eyes and breathed in deeply, noting the

heady, seductive scent of Jeremy's aftershave, of his skin. "What…what are you doing?"

"I'm seeing you better. I'm touching you and breathing you. Now what was the problem you were telling me about?"

Automatically her eyes flew open. She reached up and grasped his hands. "You're trying to distract me."

He smiled, that seductive smile. "No, I'm trying to distract *me*. I don't want to discuss the child. Yet. I've spent the past few days trying to imagine the best and the worst, trying to pray and fearing that my prayers would go unanswered, that it was already too late. In the end, all my attempts were futile, because until we find the child, I can't do a thing. I can't help or protect him or her. You were right to distract me. I was getting morose, although…"

"What?"

"Jonathan DeFray is going to have the best computer communications system possible. The job was a great time killer."

"That's good. The man is already singing your praises. Now he'll really be excited about doing business with you."

But it appeared that Jeremy wasn't listening. His attention was on her and then back on the climbing wall. "This cost you," he said.

"I was safe."

"Yes, but there's safe and then there's safe. Most spiders won't hurt humans, but plenty of people have a dreaded fear of them. You're afraid of heights, and knowing that, I would never have asked you to tackle this wall. Yet you did, because you thought I needed to be shaken out of my hole." His fingers dipped down to caress her cheek. His lips followed.

"Don't let me change you or hurt you, Eden," he said,

his mouth so close to her ear that the warmth of his breath feathered across her skin.

"I won't," she said, hoping she was telling the truth but afraid she was lying. She battled for air and sanity and control as he touched her and her body trembled. What was happening? Why did she want to lean closer when she knew she should move away? Frantic, she struggled for a way out.

"And we're going to find the child," she finally blurted out, desperate to stop thinking about how much she wanted to move closer to him. "As soon as possible. I'm helping Barry." The words helped. She pulled away and stepped back.

"You're helping Barry? Barry who has a thing for you?" Jeremy frowned. Then he blew out a breath. "You're right. That's probably a good thing. Thank you. I owe you so much. Now, let's get you out of this gear and go inside." He turned…a little bit too far to the right.

Eden glanced at him and realized what she hadn't before. She could see those fierce amber eyes clearly.

"Jeremy, you're not wearing your sunglasses." She frowned. He never went outside without them.

Grinning, he playfully touched her nose with one finger. "I was in a hurry."

Because she had been dangling on a wall ten feet in the air, perfectly safe but afraid.

"The sun…" she said. "It's exceptionally bright today. What *can* you see today under these circumstances?"

Then, even though he had moved away from her, he took two steps closer and swept his hand up her side from her thigh, dipping into the curve at her waist, up her torso, over the neckline of her shirt. His fingertips brushed her earlobe, sending a shiver of need through her entire body. Somehow she managed to keep breathing.

"You're wearing dark jeans, a light-colored knit shirt with a scoop neck, small earrings shaped like bells. And—" he leaned closer "—you smell like cinnamon toast." He slid one hand around her waist and pulled her closer, kissing her lips. "You taste like cinnamon, too, and your lips are warm." He kissed her again.

His lips were warm, too, and firm and commanding. Eden wanted more. "The scent and taste of cinnamon isn't something you can see," she said weakly.

"They are when you're nearly blind," he whispered, touching his tongue lightly to her lower lip. "This is how I see you. You look good, Eden. You look…beautiful. Stay off that wall unless I'm with you. And if you need to see me and I'm not around, next time just knock on my door. You have the right. By the way, Eden…"

"Yes?" She looked up at him, waiting.

"You were pretty spectacular up on that wall. Scared or not, you tackled the thing with an amazing spirit." And then he turned and left her there wondering what she had been thinking when she decided to entice Jeremy outside. Had she really worried about the man? How silly, when she was the one whose heart was clearly at risk and whose heart-strings were being played by a master who would move on to the next set of lips very soon.

# CHAPTER TEN

"YOU idiot, Fulton," Jeremy said the next day. Eden didn't deserve to have him toying with her or caressing her, but darn the woman, every time she was near him he forgot about all his good intentions and seemed to be losing more than his sight. His mind, his emotions and definitely his self-control were in jeopardy, as well.

A groan escaped him. Eden had actually climbed the wall to entice him outside. Could he do any less than answer the call?

"Darn woman," he muttered, but he was smiling when he said it. "Donald," he said later. "Saddle up the horses."

"Sir? Mr. Fulton?"

Jeremy winked. "I'm going to tempt Eden out on a bicycle. The poor woman needs some fresh air."

Donald chuckled. "Sure thing, Mr. Fulton. I'm sure I can find one her size."

"And, Donald?" Jeremy continued.

The man waited.

"Thank you for making sure she didn't get hurt yesterday. Next time call me."

"She's spunky, Mr. Fulton. I don't think she would have taken no for an answer."

Jeremy sighed. "You're probably right. I'm beginning to see how I drove my aunt crazy, always plunging ahead with no thought to how it would worry others."

"Eden did it for you, Mr. Fulton."

"I know. I don't deserve it. And you don't have to say the polite thing here, Donald. You've worked for me long enough to just let me mumble on."

Donald shook his head and smiled.

"So…where do you think she is, Donald?"

"Working. She's always at that computer of hers, working."

"Mmm. She definitely needs fresh air." Jeremy pulled out his cell phone and called the line to Eden's office.

"Eden Byars," she said, and her low, musical voice sent a tremor right through Jeremy.

"Meet me by the garage. Wear comfortable, casual clothes."

"Why?"

"I'm following your directions and getting out. I need…company." He just couldn't use the word *help*. Not with Eden.

"Company's coming," she said. The phone went dead.

Within minutes they were on the road. "You be the navigator," Jeremy said.

"Do I know where we're going?"

"No. And neither do I. Just ride."

She laughed. "I haven't been on a bicycle for years, but…just ride? That I can do."

Outside the gates, there was traffic, which necessitated

the two of them riding single file. "I'm turning right," Eden called to him. He could see her turn, but judging when to make his own turn was a bit more complicated. The combination of motion and traffic was energizing but also a bit disorienting, and the curb he had to round wasn't visible. "Two seconds, one, now," Eden said quietly, then continued down the road.

"I love this!" she said a few minutes later as they found a path along the lake. "I never realized what fun it was. I didn't get to do much of this when I was young."

"Too many responsibilities?" Jeremy asked.

"Partly. And the fact that I had no bike," she confided.

"Your uncle could have afforded one," he mused.

"Yes, but he thought we would start thinking we deserved more than we did if he provided us with luxuries. Eventually my brother earned enough money working at a fast-food place to buy one, and he let us share now and then."

While he could have had five hundred bikes if he'd wanted them, Jeremy couldn't help thinking.

"Jeremy!" a voice called. He turned in the general direction but there was traffic and masses of people. He couldn't tell where the sound was coming from.

"Five o'clock," Eden said, giving him directions. "Gorgeous, long, curling red hair, big brown eyes, very shapely. Likes very feminine clothing if the ruffles at her wrists and throat are anything to go by," she said softly.

"Leslie Minnival," Jeremy said. "Has to be. Is there a dog?"

"A little one. White."

But by now the woman was rushing up to them. "Jeremy, where have you been? I'd heard you were back in town for a while, but I haven't seen you around. Did you get tired of traveling the world?"

He saw Eden move to the side. She turned toward him, and he could practically feel the questions rolling off her. Ah, so Ashley hadn't told Eden that he'd been traveling until he had gotten the bad news about his eyes.

"Something like that, yes," he agreed.

"It's so good running into you. Things have been incredibly boring around here, and you always provide some spice. Hey, ladies, come see who's here."

Jeremy heard a shriek and the sound of his name being uttered. He wasn't even sure where to look as he abandoned the bike. But suddenly Eden was beside him. "Tonya Hilding," she said quietly. "It's nice to see you. And Rebecca Darien. It's been forever. Charlotte Wills, hello. I'm Eden Byars, Ashley's cousin." As she called out the women's names she unobtrusively ran a finger over Jeremy's hand. L, C, R. Left, center, right.

"Eden, of course we remember you," one of the women was saying and sounding very much as if she didn't remember at all. "It's *so* good to see you again."

But Jeremy knew this group had been part of Miriam's entourage. Eden wouldn't have been one of their favored friends.

"Eden…are *you* dating Jeremy these days?" another woman asked, an incredulous tone to her voice.

Jeremy felt Eden's body go stiff beside him. He knew what that trio would think; that he would never have dated someone like Eden.

"Oh," she said. "No."

"Yes," he said suddenly, snagging her hand and drawing

her to him. "Eden, sweetheart, I know we decided to stick to the employee story, but these are our friends. They've known us a long time. And they can see that I'm completely mad for you."

She raised her hand and cupped his jaw, but he could sense her discomfort. Her pretty face blurred a bit more as she came closer. "You're sweet to say so, but I *am* your employee."

"Yes, love, but you're also much more," he said. He slid his palm to her waist and tugged her against his body, savoring the contact as her soft flesh molded to his. He felt Eden's shock at his sudden, personal possession, but she quietly played along and melted into him.

The woman on the left, Tonya, had moved in at the right angle for him to see her. She was eyeing Eden as if wondering if she was the same Eden who had attended high school with her.

"Always on the move with the women," she said, laughing.

"Well, not so much anymore," he told her. "Eden is special, and I've grown more sophisticated in my taste as I've gotten older. I've learned to look beneath the heavy makeup, the hair extensions and the um, surgical enhancements. She doesn't need all that shallow stuff, and Eden has something that other women just don't have."

Eden was all but squirming beside him. He splayed his fingers wider, touching more of her. She stilled, despite the tension radiating from her body into his fingertips.

"Oh, well, yes," Rebecca said. "I'm so glad that's working out for you."

"Thank you," he said.

"Jeremy, we're having a party two nights from now," Charlotte was saying. "It's a charity thing, for children. We sent you an invitation and you turned us down, but we'd just love to have you. The Fulton name would mean so much."

Until some woman gazed into his eyes and realized he couldn't see all of her attributes. "Two nights from now? I'm sorry, no, but I'll send you a check," he said.

"You're sure? Eden could come, too, if you want."

Now he really was sure. No one begrudgingly offered Eden a space at the table. "A large check," he said. And he said his goodbyes and drew Eden away.

Without discussing it, they turned their bikes around and rode home.

"You could have gone. They're your friends."

"They were never my friends any more than they were yours."

Eden seemed to study that. "You're right. They're not as deep and caring as you."

He nearly choked. "Me, deep and caring?"

She stared him down. Then she reached out and touched his arm. "Don't try to pretend you're just a handsome face and a lot of muscles. I know you really will send that check, just as I know that their charity ball probably spends most of its money on food, wine and decorations and gives very little to the children. And with all the research I've been up to, I also know that you have several genuine children's charities you contribute to. One you even started yourself recently."

He frowned. "Not an unselfish move. If it were, I would have started it years ago."

She laughed. "Jeremy, probably the majority of the charities in the world began when personal tragedy struck someone and they felt a need to do something. That doesn't make the giving any less genuine. You do good."

"So do you. You helped me today."

"And you helped me."

He raised his brow. "How?"

"I know you pretended I was your girlfriend so they wouldn't remember me as I really was and look down on me."

"I didn't exactly have that deliberate a plan. I just didn't like them when they were young and I assumed they had probably once snubbed you."

"Well, they might have if they had actually noticed that I existed." She laughed again. "How did you know Charlotte had implants?" There was something in her voice that made Jeremy smile.

"I didn't. I guessed that one of them might. I certainly never touched her."

For a second he thought Eden was smiling, but then she moved away quickly, so quickly he thought he might have imagined the smile. Did Eden care if he touched other women? She knew him to be a hit-and-run lover. Did *he* care how she felt about that?

Yes, but he was going to continue to point out his character flaws, anyway. It might immunize her from hurt if he let himself get out of line.

"I'm sorry about the party, if you wanted to go," he told her.

"I would have been out of place there."

"But there's also a cocktail party I've been asked to attend by Jonathan DeFray two nights from now. Go with me," he urged.

He could sense her hesitation. "It would be a help," he told her. "There might be name tags." He said the words as if they were something from a bad horror movie.

"At a cocktail party given by Jonathan DeFray?"

"You never know."

She chuckled. "If Mr. DeFray provided them, they'd be gold plated with diamond lettering."

"See, you're conceding they might have them. I won't be able to read them. I'll be staring at some woman's breast trying to figure out who she is and get my face slapped."

"Hah! If you were staring at her breast, she'd probably just purr. You have that effect on women."

Jeremy felt a rush of heat slither through him. His whole body went on alert. Did he have that effect on Eden?

"You don't really need me," she said suddenly, emphatically. "I'll feel out of place."

Of course. She had never been thrown into the kind of situation he was talking about.

"I do need you," he said firmly. "There are so many things I can't do well anymore."

"You're still maneuvering better than most men would. You certainly nailed the hair extension thing," she said, her voice troubled. "Are you sure you should be taking me there? I wasn't invited."

"You'll be welcomed and needed. Where I go, you go, and I haven't told Jonathan that I'll be there yet. Will you go with me?"

Still she hesitated. "Is it important?"

He was tempted to lie, but he just couldn't do that with her. "I won't lose the account if I'm not there, but it would be beneficial for me to be there in terms of cementing a relationship with the firm. Jon promised 'nonstop fun.'"

Eden chuckled. "Will there be games or dancing?"

"Not sure about the games, but I'll twist Jonathan's arm until he agrees to dancing."

"Mmm, nice way to treat a client."

"Jonathan likes me. He likes you, too. We'll dance, with or without music." It occurred to him that it might be the only chance in this lifetime that he would be able to dance and still see. There were so many moments like that lately. *Is this the last time I'll see this reasonably clearly? Will what I'm seeing have disappeared into the fog tomorrow?*

Jeremy refused to give in to that kind of thinking. Besides, there was really only one important point here. This would be the one and only time he would get to dance with Eden.

"You're changing her," Ashley said to Jeremy the next day. "I spoke with her yesterday. She's laughing. She talks about bicycling and in-line skating and tennis and rock climbing. Rock climbing! Eden, who's petrified of heights."

"She was scared, but actually very good at it. No, not good. She was magical."

"You sound entranced, but then you've been entranced many times in the past."

"Is that a warning, Ashley?"

"I hope so. Is it clear? She's been hurt time and time again by people who abandoned her in various ways. My father was one of them. Not a great father, but an even worse uncle. He offered the house but nothing more. No financial or emotional support of any kind, no acknowledgment of them at birthdays or Christmas. But, he painted himself as a Good Samaritan because they lived on his land. He used them for his own purposes. So, don't you use her just because you're bored or scared that you're losing your touch or because she's one of the few people who knows your secret and having her around feels safe to you."

Was he doing that? Jeremy wanted to say no, but that was too easy.

"I don't want to hurt Eden," he said.

"And I don't want to eat too much chocolate, but I do."

"You have a point. I'm trying to be careful."

"Maybe I shouldn't have sent her to you."

"Do you want to be the person who asks her to leave before the job is done?"

"You could give her a hefty severance package."

"Ash, this is Eden we're talking about."

"Point taken. She's too honorable to take money she doesn't feel she's earned. So…what are you going to do?"

"I don't know. Stop doing some of what I'm doing?"

"What *are* you doing?" Instantly Ashley's voice was filled with suspicion.

The answer couldn't be avoided. *I'm kissing her too much. I'm dreaming of touching her every night. I'm dying to get her in my arms and in my bed. I'm not sure I'm not using her.*

"Jeremy? Answer the question."

"I'm taking a very big step back," he said. "Are you happy?"

"Not a bit. She sounded happy when I talked to her, but I was afraid it was a false happiness. If you feel the need to take a big step back, then I was right. You were on the road to hurting her."

Jeremy didn't have a good counter to that. "You always saw right through me, Ash."

"I know. That was why you and I didn't last. Well, that

and the fact that you would have dumped me, anyway, if I hadn't run first."

"You're a good friend, Ashley. Keep being a good cousin to Eden. Don't let me do something to damage her. I want her whole when she leaves here."

In a way that he *wasn't* whole, he conceded. And he wasn't talking about his eyes.

Eden? He was out of control with Eden. What was he going to do to get things back on the right path so that when she left here, she would go smiling, even if he couldn't actually see the smile on her face?

Something drastic, something that would probably make him hate himself.

# CHAPTER ELEVEN

JONATHAN'S party was a great success, Eden had to admit, even though she was feeling tense and vaguely unhappy. All week she had cruised the Web sites Barry had given her. There was a registry where donor offspring or their parents could try to make contact with their donors. She was trying that route, making connections and building bridges with people while Barry was using outside contacts and more conventional methods. He thought he might be on the trail of the child. The tension was mounting in her and in Jeremy, but that wasn't the cause of this vague feeling of dread that was suffusing her now.

"I appreciate the information and the fact that you're keeping me up to date," Jeremy had said when she'd given him a progress report. "You're an excellent assistant."

Which was a nice thing to say and yet…the unhappy feeling grew.

When some of the visual aids she had ordered had arrived, she had reluctantly delivered them to Jeremy to try them out, remembering that she had badgered him into being a guinea pig.

"I'll have a report to you in the morning," he had said.

And he had. He'd entered her office, tall and dark, imposing and utterly distant. No grin, no teasing, but he had hesitated at the door. She'd turned to him and caught a frown on his face. "You have everything you need?" he asked.

"Yes."

And yet she didn't have everything she needed at all. She missed his teasing and his smiles. Just two days ago she would have tried to coax him into sharing a laugh with her, but when she'd tried that yesterday he had given her a patient but very small smile, thanked her and then gone back to work.

*No question why,* she thought. Ashley had called two days ago. She'd offered counsel. She'd suggested caution.

"I love him. He's my friend and neighbor," Ashley had said, "but I know him too well. He has nothing permanent to offer, but he's so incredibly tempting. He knows just what to say to a woman. Even worse, he knows just how to touch a woman." Which made Eden feel awful. So many women knew his touch, but she never really would.

*That's a good thing,* she reminded herself. *You couldn't handle being just another fling for him.*

"I'm worried you're starting to fall in love with him," Ashley had continued.

It had been all Eden could do to keep from covering her ears or from running screaming from the room, but Ashley was right.

"I'll be fine," she had promised her cousin, but she wasn't fine. She was falling. Hard. With no soft cushion to land on.

"I spoke to him," Ashley said. "He agreed that he might have let things get out of control. He really likes and respects you and doesn't want to see you hurt. I made him promise to behave from now on."

The words were like stab wounds. Jeremy had admitted that he had gone overboard with her, Eden thought. As he had with other women he flirted with and then walked away from. Hadn't she learned anything from her father and husband?

"You could leave. I could find him someone else," Ashley said.

It would be smart. She'd already earned enough to pay her creditors. "I'll think about it."

But then she had come upon Jeremy in a hallway. He had been standing near a painting of a garden in front of a lake, very reminiscent of Monet. A gorgeous piece, one Eden had often thought that she could stare at for hours.

But Jeremy couldn't stare at it the way she could. He could see it, but not all of it at once. He couldn't make out the details or the subtleties. Instead he had been touching the painting and he had been embarrassed when she'd come upon him.

Still, true to form, he hadn't jerked his hand away like a guilty child, but had slowly lowered it to his side. "Probably not the best thing for the painting," he admitted.

"It's your painting," she pointed out.

"Not really. I think it still belongs to the person who created it, at least in some ways. And while an artist might want others to enjoy his work, well…I'm pretty sure touching a painting is frowned upon."

Slowly she shook her head. "Art is meant to be seen in a thousand different ways, so if the viewer owns it and senses it better with his fingertips… I embarrassed you, didn't I?"

He thought about that. "No. You don't make me feel that I'm less than I was."

The question that came to mind arrived so easily even though she knew it was the completely wrong question to ask. It was a question that should never be asked. A major part of her didn't even want to ask it, but her mouth just seemed to jump in there and take over.

"What do I make you feel?" she said.

He looked to the side. "Like a man with a fire inside him. I want to touch you. I want to taste you. And it would be the worst thing I ever did if I allowed that to happen. I like you too much to use you for my own selfish desires, knowing that when we're done here I'll walk away. I'll go back to Europe or Asia or Australia and stay away from my old life as much as I can, and you'll go back to St. Louis. We'll probably never meet again. You don't want that kind of complication in your life."

She did. At that moment she wanted to risk it all just to have him touch her, but...he was right, too. She was cowardly and she feared the pain that would follow.

"I would hurt you," he said, as if reading her mind. "You want things I'll never want and can't have. I can't do real relationships or a normal family. Heck, I'm not even sure what a normal family feels like, but I also can't be what I once was and use people anymore. I can no longer blithely pretend that I can do anything and the consequences won't matter. I'd hate myself later."

"I know. It's all right."

"No," he said. "It's not." And it wasn't.

Now they were at the party, and it was all Jonathan had said it would be. But, after her exchange with Jeremy, Eden felt miserable. Surprisingly enough, her discomfort had little to do with the rich guests who would have normally made her feel nervous, self-aware and inadequate. Tonight she was focused solely on Jeremy. And after the episode with Ashley and today's conversation, she was trying her best to remember that Jeremy was just a job.

She needed to do her job well, but not do more. So she stood as inconspicuously as possible at Jeremy's side and quietly described other guests so that he could identify them. She let him know if there was some obstacle in his way that he might not be aware of. She concocted stories about what was on the buffet table so that it wouldn't look as if she was relating something he didn't already know.

"Don't you just love these little butterfly shrimp on skewers?" she asked, reaching for one and popping it into her mouth. "Or how about these spinach rolls? Or these gorgeous little crackers with some sort of topping?" She picked up one of them. And then stopped cold.

Immediately Jeremy turned to her. "Eden?"

"I'm sorry. I—"

He drew her arm through his. "The door," he ordered. "I think we need some fresh air."

Still holding the cracker, she moved toward the open French doors and toward the edge of the huge deck. "Two stairs down," she whispered. "We're at the first one now."

Together they smoothly stepped down onto the grass and away from the crowd. When the crowd had disappeared behind them he turned to her. "What's wrong? Why did you freeze that way?"

She wrinkled her nose. "It's nothing. It's really stupid. I feel so foolish."

He tilted his head and looked at her more closely in that wonderful, sexy, lopsided way of his that always brought him nearly cheek to cheek with her. She always felt as if he might just lean forward a bit more and whisper in her ear. He might place his mouth on her, drop kisses beneath her ear, down her jaw to her throat and…

Eden caught her breath. She blinked and shook her head, fighting to slow her breathing so Jeremy wouldn't hear the change in her voice or zero in on the changes in her demeanor in that disarming way he had. She was aware of the moon shining full on her face, which might make her a bit more visible to him. "What is it that's upset you?" he finally asked.

"I…it's just…this hors d'oeuvre." She held up the cracker. "I couldn't make out what was on it when I first picked it up. It's egg. I'm totally allergic, but it was already in my hand. I didn't want to be rude and throw it away and I couldn't eat it and I really couldn't put it back on the plate after I had touched it. That would be such an ill-mannered thing for an assistant of yours to do and—"

A small chuckle slipped from Jeremy's lips. "You couldn't see it? I absolutely love that. Eden, you're wonderful, a complete delight. I bring a woman with me to be my eyes and she can't see any more than I can."

It was so good to hear him laugh again, to hear that deep, sexy rumble that Eden just couldn't help laughing, too, despite reminding herself to stick to her employee role.

"Don't make fun of me," she finally managed to say. "I spent years teaching myself the rules of society with no adult to guide me, and here I am brought low by a bit of egg." She held the cracker as if it were an explosive device.

"Ah, but I can solve your social dilemma," Jeremy said. "I'm not allergic to eggs." And he bent closer. He placed his hand beneath hers and lifted her fingertips to his lips, stealing the small bite from her grasp. His lips and his tongue touched her. "Problem solved," he said.

With the greatest of efforts she withheld her moan. "Nice magic trick," she said. "Why didn't I just think of feeding you? You are, after all, a man. And with all the exercise you get, you tend to be a human eating-machine."

His chuckle was warm. His smile charmed her. "I'm glad to be of help, my lovely Cinderella," he said with a mock bow. "In spite of your insulting remarks about my eating habits, I'm yours to command should the need arise again." And his smile turned into a full-fledged look of total amusement.

"I've really missed you," she said without even thinking. "I've missed your laugh."

Instantly his gaze turned hot and fierce. "I explained all that."

"I know, and you're right," she said with a resigned sigh. "But no matter the problems, I *do* have to spend time with you in order to get from point A to point B. I'm supposed to be helping you. I'm your employee."

A harsh laugh escaped him. "That's only a partial truth, Eden. You're a bit more than my employee."

And there it was. The very thing she had been fighting. This couldn't be a simple, safe, risk-free employer-employee relationship and there had never really been a chance of that. At least on her part.

"Maybe that's true. There's no getting past the fact that we both know I once had a horrible crush on you. But we're not kids anymore. I'm not sobbing over my pet. And, yes, I've already admitted that I'm still attracted to you, but I'm doing an okay job of ignoring my attraction. I know darn well it wouldn't be smart to indulge myself, not when you're—"

She couldn't say the words.

"When *I'm* a man who *isn't* doing an okay job of ignoring his attraction. The fact is that my temperature rises every time you're in the room," he said. "I want to see what's under this soft, silky thing you're wearing. I want to place my hands on you and feel what I can't see."

Eden's heart was beating so fast that she was afraid she might pass out. Instead she forced herself to raise her chin. "Yes, but we've both admitted that that's mere physical attraction. It's natural to feel that way given the amount of time we're together. And, I think…it's okay as long as we're both aware that this is going nowhere. Neither of us wants it to get out of hand, but can't we still be—I don't know. Business associates *and* friends? This arrangement was friendly for a while. For the short time we're going to be working together, can't we try to get back to that?"

His smile was thin. He blew out a long breath and muttered a word beneath his breath that she had never heard him use. "Are you sure you heard what I said and that you understand the impending difficulties of our arrangement?"

"Yes," she said solemnly. "You want to sleep with me, but you won't."

Jeremy groaned. "That was such a schoolteacher tone, so matter-of-fact."

She shrugged. "It's who I am," she said casually, although she wasn't feeling anything even close to casual.

"You want me to agree to be friends?"

"And business associates. Let me go back to just being a good employee again."

Jeremy studied the sky he couldn't see clearly. Then he laughed a bit harshly. "Who knew that I would ever develop a conscience?"

Maybe they *could* go backward, Eden thought. Maybe she could get over him if they tried to turn back the clock. "Friends?" she asked again.

"Did anyone ever tell you that you're very persistent?"

"Had to be. I had to feed and raise a bunch of kids."

He nodded. "All right. Friends. And for the record, I missed you, too."

"That's because we're biking buddies."

He gave her a look. No, he gave her *the* look, the one that said that biking wasn't what he most wanted to do with her.

"Okay, I won't push it," she said.

Jeremy laughed. "You always push." And then he reached down and took her hand. "You wanted to know if there would be dancing at this party. There is."

He pulled her into his arms and they moved over the uneven ground. Jeremy had clearly been dancing from birth, because his steps were faultless. Eden, who had never been an accomplished dancer, knew that she wouldn't fall as long as he was holding her. It was heaven. Very temporary heaven, she amended.

They were friends again, even though she was feeling something more than friendship, something she didn't want to think about.

*And I won't think about it,* she told herself. *I can be careful for just a few more weeks.*

"It's a boy," Barry said, the minute he walked into the room the next day.

Jeremy felt all the blood drain from his face. He had

fathered a child. He'd known that for days. Now he knew more.

"Where? Who?" he asked. He avoided looking at Eden. He did his best to keep his expression calm so that she wouldn't see how much this was affecting him.

"I don't know, yet. Another employee of the agency saw one of my messages. She remembered you and the mother and she said she was relatively certain that the child was yours. She might have more information soon."

Jeremy's heart was pounding fast. Panic threatened even as he pushed it away.

His eyesight was getting worse. When he had looked at Eden last evening and held her while they danced, there had been...less of her even as his feelings were growing more powerful.

"All right, keep at it," he said casually. He turned to Eden. "Progress of sorts," he said, and he actually managed to smile.

"I'm glad," she said.

And now? A real child with a past and a future and dreams that could easily be shattered. What could he do about that? he asked himself later when he was alone in his room.

But the world felt dark and the answers wouldn't come. He knew all too much about loss and injustice. Sometimes the sins of adults were paid for by children.

"And sometimes you end up hoping all your life not to be like your father but in the end, you *are* him," Jeremy said. A person whose careless, selfish deeds kept punishing others.

The only bright light in this scenario was that he hadn't given way to temptation and taken advantage of Eden. She was still relatively unharmed.

# CHAPTER TWELVE

EDEN tried to concentrate on work, but nothing was getting done. She couldn't stop thinking about how Jeremy had tried to hide his concern when Barry had told him about the child.

Giving up, Eden left the library and returned to the cottage. She wandered the rooms a much-younger Jeremy had once wandered. He had come here when he was upset.

He was upset now. And she remembered how he had once comforted her in her distress. She knew he wouldn't want her to reciprocate.

She should try to distract herself. Reading would be good. Eden scanned the shelves of books she'd studied before. Kipling. Terry Pratchett. Stephen King. Hermann Hesse. Vonnegut. There was plenty to choose from, but her hand strayed to the one tome she had forbidden herself to look at. It was so innocent looking and yet…Eden's hand shook when she reached for it. She pulled away.

A journal of some sort. The corners were damaged and looked as if they had been wet at one time. Had it been Jeremy's? Was it another one of those things his aunt had tossed and Lula had rescued and returned recently?

"If it was, it's none of your business," she told herself.

"You can't look." She picked it up, prepared to put it with the photos she had found earlier, out of harm's way and out of sight so that there would be no question of prying or guilty glances.

But as she did, a bit of paper fell to the floor, something that had been sandwiched between the journal and the book next to it.

Eden picked up the paper and found herself staring at an old newspaper clipping of a woman who bore a striking resemblance to Jeremy. The caption under the photo was incomplete, but Eden clearly saw the words Jemma Fulton, engaged to be married to Peter Bowers. Half the clipping was ripped away.

And Jeremy's name was Fulton, not Bowers. What had happened?

"None of your business," she told herself again. And yet, whatever had happened then was still affecting Jeremy today. It was the reason he was who he was and why he felt such a great guilt about her and about the child.

With only the slightest hint of conscience, Eden flipped on her computer monitor. Whatever had happened had been a long time ago, but the Fultons were a significant family. They were news. Perhaps if she knew more…

In a short while she did know more. She also knew that she should leave well enough alone.

But she couldn't do that.

Getting up, she went out into the dark and crossed to the mansion. She let herself into the quiet building and climbed the curving staircase to the second floor where only Jeremy stayed.

There were twelve bedrooms, but she knew which

was his. Her heart clenched, her mouth was dry, and she was shaking.

She should leave, but he was up here alone, condemning himself. Eden approached the door and knocked softly. She heard a muttered curse.

"It's me. Eden," she said, and the door opened. He stood there, his white shirt open all the way, chest bared, his longish hair a bit wild, like some modern-day Heathcliff. But not Heathcliff. Nothing like the brooding fictional brute.

Jeremy. She thought the word, and then she said it.

"You shouldn't be here," he said. "I'm not in control right now."

"I don't care." She held out the clipping, took his hand and led his fingers to it. "I'm sorry. I found the picture of your mother. I nosed around and read some snippets about her. Your father was in this photo, wasn't he?"

Jeremy's expression was practically a snarl. "Did you read what he did?"

"You told me. About jilting your aunt."

He laughed, a harsh sound. "That wasn't all."

"I didn't think it was."

"And you want to know the rest. All the ugly truth."

"I want to come in," she said on a shaky breath.

"That wouldn't be wise."

"I'm aware of that, but I still want to come in. And then, yes, I want you to tell me the rest of the story."

He looked to the side, the anger clearly simmering just beneath the surface. "I'm surprised at you, Eden. I never took you for the nosy type."

"Well, I am. When necessary."

"And you think it's necessary for you to know all my dirty, little secrets?"

"No, but in this case, yes."

He raised a brow. He still hadn't invited her in. "Why?"

And now came the hard part. "You're always warning me about yourself. You're the big bad wolf and I'm apparently Bo Peep. But that's never really stopped me, partially because you've always been a mystery. I have a fascination with you and apparently it's a bit mutual."

"A bit," he agreed with a grim look.

"I think…I think that if there's complete openness between us, then all the little mysteries we built up as teenagers will disappear. Because, despite all the bad things you and others have related about your past, my infatuation persists. I think I began to realize that when we were talking about Cinderella."

"You keep expecting me to turn into a prince."

"Not exactly, but…sort of. And you think I might have a glass slipper in my future, that I'm more interesting than I am."

Okay, he did smile then.

"Jeremy, the child…it was so unavoidable. I hate that you blame yourself for that."

Now he was shaking his head. He took her hand and drew her farther into the room, closing the door behind her. "Eden," he said, reaching out and cupping her jaw with his hand. "I knew you came here tonight to help me. All that stuff about getting over your infatuation was a ruse."

"A little, maybe, but it's also absolutely true," she said. "I hate the fact that I still have a crush on you. I don't want to want you."

He took a deep breath. "Good. But you did have some humanitarian plan, too, didn't you?"

"I don't know. Maybe. Okay, yes. I just don't want you to feel such a burden and to have to carry it alone. Believe me, I know about those kinds of things. Sometimes, in my mother's more lucid moments, I *know* she felt guilt that she couldn't care for her children, and the guilt only made things worse."

"Because then you tried to take some of the guilt from her."

Eden frowned. "I'm no saint. I was angry most of the time. There were babies who needed their mother, but...my father had abandoned her. He shouldn't have left her that way, and my uncle should have been more helpful."

"Men *haven't* been nice to you, have they?"

"No, but those men are gone, so I don't have that problem anymore." Except for the danger of wanting Jeremy, another man who would, inevitably, fail her if she asked for the impossible.

"All right, I'll tell you what you came here to find out," he said. "You know about my father and my aunt. He got my mother pregnant and got engaged to her, but then he never actually married her. He jilted her just the way he jilted my aunt. I'm a Fulton in fact, not just because my mother chose to keep her maiden name. She wasn't given a choice. Both the Fulton women were betrayed by the same man. I sometimes wonder if my aunt wasn't a different person before him. The incident destroyed her relationship with my mother."

Eden hesitated. "You think you're like him, don't you?"

"In ways I am. I've certainly hurt people in the way he did, by not following through or being able to commit. At least I admit that much. I'm not sure he did. He just kept hurting people. There were times it was probably uninten- tional, but it still happened and people's lives were changed."

Jeremy was one of those, Eden knew. Money and a big house couldn't take away shame, the loss of a parent or the indignities that followed. She knew that so well.

Against her will, tears began to slide down her cheeks.

"Eden?" Jeremy stroked his finger over her jaw, and the tears dampened his skin. "Eden, you're breaking my heart. I wish you had had a more perfect childhood," he said gently. "I wish, back when I had the chance, that I could have been more sensitive or knowledgeable and made things better for you."

She shook her head. "I'm okay with my past. I want you to be okay with yours."

He kissed her palm, and she leaned into his touch. "Still nurturing others, Eden?"

Eden couldn't breathe, could barely think. "I never met your father, but you can't make me believe you're like him. And I don't want you to blame yourself for the child."

He froze at that. "We'll see. I have to find out more about him first. Let's take this one step at a time."

All right, she knew she wasn't going to win on this one. "Jeremy?"

"Yes?" he said, stroking his hand over her head, his fingers tangling in her hair.

"I lied about wanting to know about your father. I already knew all of it. I got nosy and looked it all up online."

She felt his smile.

"You're not angry?"

"No."

"You should be. I invaded your privacy."

"You did it for a good cause. You seem to be a bit of a crusader. I seem to be your current project. I've accepted that."

She sighed and leaned against him.

"But you should go," he told her. "Because we're in my bedroom with your palm against my naked chest, and I'm just not strong enough to resist that kind of temptation."

Eden looked at where her palm touched his skin in the golden light from the lamp on the bedside table. Longing overtook her. Couldn't she have something for herself just one time?

"I'll be gone soon, Jeremy," she said, swallowing hard. "I…I'll spend the rest of my life wondering what it would have been like. I want this."

He closed his eyes and his body tensed. A groan escaped him. She felt his chest rise and fall beneath her fingertips.

"I don't think you really mean that," he finally said, his voice deeper than usual. "Nighttime has a way of making people take irrational, unwise steps. You'll feel different come morning. And I'll feel—"

She leaned forward and lightly pressed her lips to his. "Don't say it. Guilt isn't going to be any part of this. We both know the rules. We're not going to have a future together. We want different things in life and our feet are set on different paths, but the past seems to color everything we say and do. I don't want to keep thinking about yesterday when tomorrow is all we can control. I know we have no future, Jeremy, but…could we have a tonight? Then I won't ever again have to wonder what I missed."

"Eden…" He reached out and caught her close, then in

two quick steps moved forward and tumbled her gently down onto the bed. He came down over her, above her, his lips close but not touching.

"Tell me you're sure," he said.

"Never more sure."

"Tell me you won't hate me in the morning."

She placed his hand over her lips and smiled. "I could never hate you," she said against his skin.

"I've fought this so long, it's hard to stop fighting."

Eden stilled. "I don't want to force you, Jeremy."

And with that he tilted his head back and laughed. "You amaze me, constantly. You enchant me. And you make me very...hot." He leaned close and nipped lightly at her neck.

Heat sluiced through her body. She moaned. Her arms came up to twine around his neck. *Love me,* she wanted to say, but she bit her lip. "Kiss me. Make love to me," she said instead.

Jeremy took her in his arms. He peeled her clothing away and exposed her skin inch by inch. He kissed her, everywhere.

Then he shrugged out of his shirt and the rest of his clothes. Taking her in his arms, he kissed her deeply.

"Tell me to stop now if you've changed your mind."

With his body against hers, she could barely think. She reached up and twined her arms about him. "Just tonight," she said. "Please."

A low growl escaped Jeremy. He kissed her again. And when he joined his body to hers, the world tipped over. It turned bright, and heat suffused her body. Desire climbed and climbed and climbed until she thought she would break or ignite. She cried his name as he touched her again, and she lost control completely. Pleasure ripped through her and she rose and fell on a tide of blissful sensation.

With the tremors still rocking her, she held him in her arms.

He kissed her under her jaw. "No regrets," he said sleepily.

"None," she promised. And when she crawled from his bed later, leaving him smiling in his sleep, she didn't regret. Yet.

She had finally had what she'd always wanted. A night in Jeremy's arms. It was all she could have of the man, and now she had to get on with her work and look forward, not back to what could never be.

Loss, pain and regrets were bound to follow…as she had known they would. But that would be later.

Jeremy woke with the summer flower scent of Eden on his pillow and the memory of her in his arms. Her kiss was imprinted on his body in a hundred places, and his vision of last night was more wonderful than he could ever have imagined.

But he swept his hand out across the bed and confirmed what his senses had already told him. She was gone.

*One night,* his own personal Cinderella had said. *We're not going to have a future together,* she had told him. *I don't want you to blame yourself* had been her words. About the lovemaking, about the past and about the child.

And a man couldn't spend the night feeling guilt when he held a beautiful, desirable woman in his arms, could he?

He frowned. It wasn't that he doubted that Eden had wanted to make love with him. She was a passionate woman, but she had also wanted to help him, to make him forget his pain. Given their earlier conversation, he was sure of that, and he had known that even as he joined his body to hers.

Who had ever helped Eden or taken an interest in her needs?

*I will,* he thought, and took Eden's advice to think about tomorrow and what could be done, not what couldn't be changed.

So…what *could* he do for her? What could he give her?

"Freedom." He whispered the word. He could give her freedom from worry about her future and about him. And maybe he could do one thing more. A simple thing, but the kind of thing that would mean something to a woman like Eden.

He tried to ignore the fact that one thing couldn't be changed. Eden would walk out of his life someday soon, and when she went, he had to pretend that he was happy. It apparently hurt her when he wasn't happy.

He grimaced. "So, I'll pretend," he said.

# CHAPTER THIRTEEN

DURING the next week, several pieces of mail were forwarded to Eden. A receipt told her that her debts were paid in full. A notice from her school reminded her that an inservice day was scheduled soon. With the clock ticking, she dove into the work of helping Barry find Jeremy's recipient child. She hunted for helpful information to make the future brighter for all parties concerned. She located and printed out first-person accounts of people who had already traveled the path Jeremy was traveling and managed to keep their lives reasonably whole. Contacting those people and asking them questions became her mission. She drove herself constantly at a feverish pace in a race to beat the clock. And to stop herself from admitting that her feelings for Jeremy were intensifying.

*Don't ever tell him that, Byars,* she ordered herself. *The man would never forgive himself for touching you.*

She had barely finished that thought when the doorbell rang. There was no one else around, so she answered it.

Immediately her mood plunged.

"Miriam," she said, staring at the beautiful, heartless woman. "I'm sorry. He's out."

For a moment a hard, bitter look crossed Miriam's face. Then her shoulders seemed to sag. "Is he really out? He never seems to be around when I come here."

"I'm sorry, yes. He is," Eden said, and for once she felt sorry for the woman. She knew just how Miriam felt.

Miriam bit her lip. Eden noticed that the woman's lipstick had smudged. She looked...sad.

"It's me, isn't it?" Miriam said. "He doesn't want to see me. Because I am what I am. A failed, twice-divorced debutante. I'm not good enough. I'm not right." Her face crumpled. A tear slipped down, marring her mascara.

And Eden suddenly realized that she no longer felt inadequate in the company of women like Miriam. Somehow this summer, without ever noticing, she'd lost that feeling that had hounded her all her life.

"I don't think it's that at all, Miriam," she said, trying to soothe the woman who had always taunted and criticized her. What she was telling Miriam was the truth, Eden realized. The problem wasn't that Miriam wasn't good enough.

*And I was always good enough, too,* she thought. *I just didn't realize it before. I spent a lifetime feeling self-conscious and awkward around the people I grew up with when the problem wasn't with me at all.* Her transformation had been Jeremy's doing. His belief in her and his complete trust in her ability to handle any situation, social or otherwise, had given her confidence and changed her in ways her education and experience hadn't. She'd told him she was his equal that first day, but that had been half bluster and half necessity. Now there was no doubt in her mind. She *was* equal, no less than Miriam or the others just because she hadn't been born into their social class.

"Jeremy just isn't looking for what you want him for, Miriam," she said gently. "He's a wonderful man, but he just isn't available. That's sad, I know. We all want him," she said, trying to tease.

Miriam blinked. "You admit that you want him?"

Eden shrugged. "What woman doesn't? Why lie about it?"

"No, I guess you're right. He *is* tempting, though, isn't he?"

"Extremely," Eden managed to say with a smile.

Miriam sighed, looking older than her years. She looked like a woman who had been beaten up. "I should go," she said, but she hesitated. "You're nicer than I thought you were."

"Well, we never really knew each other, did we?"

For a second Miriam looked guilty. "No, we didn't. Maybe we will now. If you stay."

"That would be nice," Eden said as she bade the woman goodbye. She wondered if there were depths to Miriam she hadn't seen before. Maybe. Most people hid a lot behind a veneer. Jeremy was the perfect example of a man with hidden depths.

And an example of a man no woman could keep, Eden reminded herself. But he'd given her a great deal. He'd treated her as an equal and had insisted that others treat her the same. Now she was comforting Miriam DeAngeles, a woman who had once made her feel so inadequate that she would cross the street to keep from meeting her. Jeremy had worked a minor miracle.

But now? She had to finish her work here without re-vealing just how painful it would be to leave Jeremy. She didn't want him pitying her the way she pitied Miriam. She definitely never wanted to show up on Jeremy's doorstep asking to borrow an imaginary cup of sugar.

Eden put her head down and went back to work.

"You have to stop. You're going to make yourself ill."

Eden looked up and Jeremy made no attempt to soften his expression. He was worried about her.

"I'm making progress."

"It'll get done."

"But not as quickly if I slow down. The school year is coming up fast."

All right, he saw what the situation was. She was eager to be gone. That night together had been enough to satisfy her while he wanted her more intensely than ever.

*Don't react,* he told himself. He had no business letting his masculine pride be injured when he'd spent years slipping away after only one night with a woman. If Eden needed to be gone, he'd help her…just as soon as he completed the task he'd set for himself. If everything went as planned, she would have one good thing to remember from this summer.

"I'm having a gathering in two days. I'd like you to be there," he said.

That got her attention. She lifted her head and turned toward him, her light scent curling around him, making him ache. "You need my help?" she asked, and he didn't wonder at the surprise in her voice.

"I know we haven't spent too much time together lately." Ever since the day Barry had dropped his bombshell and Eden had come to his bed, Jeremy thought. "But yes, I need your help. I can't make this affair work without you, in fact."

For a second he sensed tension in her expression and in her body. That wasn't acceptable. Just as quickly she relaxed. Was that deliberate, an act? He couldn't tell.

"Just tell me when," she said. "Tell me what you need."

*You. Now. Always.* The words were automatic. He held on until the urge to pull her to him and tell her the truth subsided a bit. "The day after tomorrow. In the gardens at eight o'clock at night. Wear something casual but festive."

"Will there be a lot of guests?"

"I hope so."

She blinked at that. "Is there anything else I should know?"

*Yes. I love you and I would never hurt you by saddling you with the responsibility of a failing man when you've lived your whole life taking care of other people's problems. I'd never keep you from your dreams.* He gave her a tight smile. "Just bring your party attitude."

For a second she looked down but he could tell that she was smiling. "Ah, another version of 'Let's get this party started,'" she said, referring to their conversation the day of the interview. "Will there be dancing?"

And then he couldn't hold back. He took her hand and kissed the palm. "Eden, there will always be dancing when you're there. I guarantee it."

He smiled back at her, even though a lance was impaling his heart. Because, of course, the problem was that Eden wouldn't always be there.

Eden stepped into the gardens wearing a white sundress with a narrow pale pink ribbon tied under her breasts.

Eight o'clock, Jeremy had said, and yet the gardens

seemed too quiet for a gathering. Had she heard him wrong? Should she go back inside?

As if he'd heard her thoughts, he appeared on a side path and held out his arm. "You look lovely," he said. "Don't ask how I can tell. I just can, especially since you always look lovely."

She placed her hand on his sleeve. "Where is everyone?" she asked. "Is it—are you and I meeting here so that you can brief me before we go inside?"

Looking up, she caught his devastating smile. "Something like that," he agreed. "Some preliminary explanations *are* necessary."

Eden nodded. "I didn't bring my notepad."

"That's good. You know I hate that thing."

"It helps me."

He tilted his head. "You said you didn't always write on it."

"It helps me focus when I need to. So…who are the guests today? Are they important?"

"Some of the most important I've ever had."

Eden suppressed a smile. "There was a time not so long ago when that would have made my knees shake."

"But not now?"

She shook her head. "Not now." And there was wonder in her voice. "I have you to thank for that. You've never treated me any differently from the way you treat everyone else. Because of that, the people who used to be so lofty and intimidating don't worry me anymore. They seem… human. Just like me."

Jeremy laughed. "That's because they are. Human, that is. I don't think anyone is just like you."

His voice deepened, and Eden's breath caught in her throat. It would be wrong and foolish to hope he was doing more than being polite when Jeremy was always polite to everyone. As Ashley had implied, it would be dangerous to want too much. "Shall we go inside?" she asked.

Jeremy captured her hand. "Not yet. I need to ask you something. You need to assist me a bit."

She stood silently and looked up at him, turning to face him. In a summer-white jacket with his longish hair falling over his forehead and his eyes studying her with something that looked a lot like anticipation, he had never looked more maddeningly handsome. Eden hoped she could remember everything he was going to tell her. Right now she felt a bit faint. Jeremy seemed to be all she could concentrate on.

"Tell me how," she said, trying to get her mind to function.

"All right, but first a question. What day is your birthday?"

She blinked. "April second. It was on the paperwork I filled out when I first came here, but…I…of course, you wouldn't have bothered reading that since you knew me. Is it important?"

He smiled and touched her cheek. "Tonight, surprisingly so. I missed your birthday."

"It's okay. I wasn't here then."

"And you won't be here for your next one, either."

"No." A lump formed in her throat.

"Then we'll have to make amends. Ashley told me that your uncle never acknowledged your birthdays or Christmas. I never did like that man."

The lump began to grow. "It's okay. I'm all grown up and he's gone now. I handle my own birthdays. My sisters call me."

Jeremy frowned. For a second he looked away. "You'd think that the sisters you raised would make a greater effort," he said, his voice a little loud as he continued to frown.

A sound she couldn't identify came from Eden's right. Whispering? Donald must be in the garden, she thought. No wonder Jeremy was frowning, if he thought they were having a private conversation.

"Don't be mad at Donald," she said. "He's such a nice man and I'm sure he didn't know we were here."

"Excuse me?" Now Jeremy looked even more confused than she felt.

"The whispering," she explained.

"Oh, yes. Donald," he said with a wide grin. "He *is* a nice man. He helped me with this. So did Mrs. Ruskin and Lula. Spruced up the gardens, made phone calls, sent out faxes and e-mails, made the cake…"

"The cake?"

"That's our cue." The whispering solidified. "Surprise!"

Eden jumped as Jeremy took her arm and led her two steps to the first turn in the garden. "Surprise, Eden!" multiple voices called.

She looked from the tables set up by the fountain. There were her sisters, all of them. And Ashley as well as Fran, Kay and Robin, three friends and fellow teachers from St. Louis. Donald, Mrs. Ruskin and Lula were standing by, wreathed in smiles.

"Happy next year's birthday, Eden," Jeremy whispered, leaning to give her a kiss on the cheek.

"I don't understand," she said, shaking her head.

He touched her cheek. "I'm taking your advice and looking forward, not back, doing what should have been done for you a long time ago. I'm thanking you for everything you've done and all you are. What's more, I'm definitely planning on dancing with you and enjoying a day with you away from work. It's been a long time since I've been to a party that wasn't work related, so I guess I owe you for this, as well."

And then, before she had time to say anything else, her friends and family came forward. "Jeremy is right," her sister Helena said. "The girls and I should have thrown you a party a long time ago. You always tried to make our birthdays special even when we didn't have any money."

Quick tears filled Eden's eyes. She turned to Jeremy to thank him, but he was on the other side of the fountain talking to Ashley. Her thanks would have to wait.

*That man,* she thought. *That surprising, wonderful man!* At a time when the tension in the house had been rising and she'd been worried out of her mind over him, he had turned the tables on her and done this. All because he'd heard she'd never had a birthday party. What would he do next?

Eden hoped it wasn't anything too wonderful. She was already in love with him. Leaving him was already going to be agony.

*She loved him…so much.* The truth hit her full force. Intense pleasure at Jeremy's gesture warred with tremendous pain. But she held her smile. Even if Jeremy couldn't see it, he could sense it, she knew. And nothing was going to spoil his joy in giving her this day. Not if she could help it.

No one was going to learn about his blindness, either. Not even her family. His pride meant so much to him. She would keep his secret, no matter what.

\* \* \*

The day was nearly over, Jeremy thought as Eden gave the last sisters hugs and saw them out the door.

"Thank you for coming," he said to Eden's youngest sister.

She bopped him on the arm. "You are a gem. Finally, someone taking care of Eden instead of the other way around."

"Karen, stop hitting my boss," Eden said. "And he is not supposed to be taking care of me. He pays me well and treats me with respect. That's all that's required."

Jeremy grinned and winked at Karen. "Eden's a bit ob-sessive about taking care of others."

Karen laughed. "Don't I know it! Has she moved your glass away from the edge of the table yet?"

"All the time," he lied. "She can drive a man crazy." Which was, of course, not a lie. "Somehow I survive," he said affectionately.

"I didn't really know you when we lived here, but I like you, Jeremy," Karen said, and Eden's other sisters agreed. "Don't work her too hard, will you? Summer's her only time to rest. I don't know why she took a job. Be good to her."

Jeremy murmured a promise. He moved away so that Eden could say goodbye to her sisters in private. As he turned to go inside, he heard Karen's whisper and saw a blur as she seemed to be gesturing in his direction.

Automatically, his spine stiffened as he wondered if his slower-than-normal movements around obstacles, his off-centered way of looking at people and his gaffes had betrayed his limitations tonight. He felt self-conscious and he realized that this must be how Eden had felt all the time she had been growing up here. Different, conspicuous, pitied.

But she'd told him just tonight that he'd helped her overcome that feeling by treating her the way he treated everyone else. He realized that she'd taken to holding her head higher lately, not shying away from the wealthy locals or worrying that people might pity her.

*What an amazing woman. He could probably learn from her.* It was something to think about.

Later. Right now there was something else bothering him. When Eden's family had gone, he took her by the elbow and turned her to face him.

"They don't know about your financial difficulties?"

He didn't have to struggle to see if Eden was frowning. Of course, she was. "It wasn't their affair. I didn't want them to worry."

"They're adults now. They could be giving you their support."

"I know they're adults, but they have their own problems." And she didn't even say that she would tell her sisters about her problems someday. It was clear that she'd never tell them or ask for assistance, but of course, *she* could be counted on to help others anytime help was needed.

That was when Jeremy realized that Eden would always take on the problems of those she cared about. Even when they were away from her. What that meant was…

Anger and frustration welled up in him. He ran his hands up her arms, and she shivered. He pulled her to him and kissed her, a hard kiss he fought to restrain. He pulled back when he wanted to move ahead and claim her.

"When you're gone," he said. "My problems will *not* be yours. I don't want you to worry about me. Ever."

"I know that you don't," she said, and there was a

sadness in her voice. That was when he discovered one more thing about Eden and himself. When she left here she *would* worry…unless he convinced her that he would be leading a perfectly fine and happy life. That meant he had to do things he hadn't anticipated doing, things he really didn't want to think about yet.

No matter. He would do them. But not tonight.

"We didn't dance," he said.

"I know. It was too busy. Would you dance with me now, please?"

"Nothing could stop me." And he swirled her into his arms. They danced in the empty gardens. He held her as close as he could.

"Jeremy, what you were saying…when we're done, when I'm gone…"

"Shh, not yet."

But soon. Barry had hinted at a breakthrough and then Eden would go home. She had a life and plans that she was eager to get back to. And tomorrow he would do what was necessary to ensure that when she left, he would never trouble her thoughts.

Eden sat at her desk and tapped out a message to the donor registry, sending it on its way. She thought of the wonderful gift Jeremy had given her and realized that it was the only birthday celebration the two of them would ever share.

"Don't think about it. Just do what you have to do," she ordered herself, but she knew that was impossible. She was missing him already.

As if in response to her thoughts, a knock sounded at

the door, and Jeremy poked his head inside. "Care to strap on your skates and go for a spin with me?"

Immediately Eden pushed back from the desk. She and Jeremy hadn't gone out together since the time they had made love. This might be their last time.

"I wouldn't miss it," she said.

Ten minutes later she placed her hand in his much larger one and they started down the lane. She breathed in deeply and sighed.

"Something wrong?" he asked, concern in his voice.

"No. Something's right. I've missed these excursions. I never used to like letting people see me in situations where I might stumble or look awkward. Now I don't worry about all that. I just love the wind in my hair." *And touching you,* she thought. "I think maybe you've created a monster."

Suddenly he spun until he was skating backward, holding both her hands. Her heart beat faster.

"You're the nicest monster I've ever met."

She laughed. "Met a lot of monsters, have you?"

"More than you know. Are you really enjoying yourself?"

"I am. More than *you* know. Thank you for showing me that I can be and do more than I thought I could."

He stopped suddenly, letting her slide forward against him. "Last night, when you were saying goodbye to your sister, she looked at me and…"

Eden's throat hurt. "Yes, she noticed something. I won't lie. But she thought you were just being coy and…oh, like a typical rich guy by not looking directly at people. We grew up with so many people avoiding eye contact with us that she didn't think too much of it."

"And you didn't tell her the truth."

Eden frowned. She stared up at him. "I wouldn't do that."

Jeremy raised a hand and traced a finger down her cheek. Heat seared her skin. The desire to lean closer was almost more than she could bear.

"I can't let you cover for me anymore. You've done everything I've asked of you. You've kept my secret and allowed me to hide, and you've even forced yourself into uncomfortable situations again and again." He gestured down toward her skates.

"I told you that I love skating and biking and—"

"You didn't always," he said. "But you did them anyway. And you stayed with me and did your part in the presence of people who made you uncomfortable."

"Yes, but—"

"Shh," he said, placing two fingers over her lips. "I know. You don't feel uncomfortable around them anymore. The butterfly has broken out of her cocoon. Your willingness to force yourself outside your comfort zone has taught me a lesson, Eden. I can't let you continue to hide my secret anymore and I can't keep avoiding unpleasant truths just to protect my pride. It's something I've been doing all my life, not just these past months, and it's time to stop. I'm going to come clean. Publicly. I want you to be with me. And then…"

She waited, her heart pounding in deep, painful thuds. She licked her lips and swallowed. "And then?" she said as calmly as she could manage.

Carefully, Jeremy loosened his hold on her. "Then I'll let you go back to your own life. We'll end it."

His words were like a wrecking ball. She'd known the day was coming. Just not yet, and…she still wasn't prepared. Her heart still shattered.

Somehow she managed to nod and smile. "All right. What do you need me to do?"

It seemed as if a long time passed before he spoke. "I'll call a public meeting, a press conference and invite a few other guests, people who should know. Colleagues and people from the business community. Just stay with me until then. Until I make the announcement. In case something unexpected happens, I'd like an intelligent, calm person to be on hand. Can you stay?"

*I can stay forever,* she wanted to say. But that wasn't what he wanted.

"Yes," she promised.

Just this last appearance together and then she would go home. Such a simple plan. But as Eden left Jeremy in the garden she knew that her life after him would not be simple or easy. She had to survive loving him and losing him. And she didn't have a clue how to do that.

Jeremy waited until he was sure that Eden had gone. Fighting for the control of his emotions that had sustained him all his life, he lost the battle. He slammed his fist into the nearest tree, ignoring the pain. It had been all he could do not to grab Eden, hold her, kiss her and beg her to stay.

He loved her, he wanted her, and he was becoming what he had feared all along, a pathetic excuse of a man who would put his own desires above those of others.

*She made love with me. Surely she cares.* The words shot through his brain and he heard the voices of all the women who had said similar things about him. And he had never cared. At least not in the way they had wanted him to.

Now he had to face the truth. Eden had spent her whole

life caring for other people who couldn't care for themselves. She'd had to clean up other people's messes and take care of other people's problems. For once in her life, she was going to have life on her terms. And she would have the children she wanted, too, the ones he couldn't give her. He would chain himself to the desk before he would do anything that would interfere with her dreams.

Whether this job was completed or not, it was time to let people in on the truth and move on. Alone.

# CHAPTER FOURTEEN

EDEN was sitting at her desk with tears threatening when the message appeared on her screen. "I'm Alisson August. My son is the result of donor 465. I understand the donor may be a problem."

Instantly Eden was alert and tense. Her hands shook as she stared at the stark, black words on the white screen. Jeremy, a problem? Any child would be lucky to have him for a donor, she wanted to say, but of course, a parent might not see things that way.

She thought for a minute. Then she began to type. Alisson August responded.

The correspondence continued into the night. It was late by the time Eden left her computer. A sense of elation warred with the knowledge that this was the last step, almost the last thing she would do for Jeremy. Her heart clenched.

But her own impending loss couldn't matter right now. She had information she had to share. Contacting Barry, she had the briefest of conversations to call him off. "We'll talk more later," she said. Then she went in search of Jeremy.

The door to his office was open. The room was empty. She

tried the bedroom. Also empty, the bed where they had made love a silent reminder of what could never happen again.

Finally she found Donald, who directed her to the garden.

Jeremy was leaning against a metal trellis, one hand in his pocket, the other holding a phone. When he realized she was there, he ended the call. "Eden," he said, a smile transforming his face. "You're a nice break from business."

He looked so…Jeremy. Eden's heart flipped. It hurt to even see him, now that the end was so near.

She still hadn't spoken, and Jeremy's smile disappeared. "Are you all right?" Concern rolled off of him. He left the trellis and came toward her.

No, she was completely crazy right now. Confused and in love and in pain. So very happy for him and yet howling inside at the inevitable final curtain.

"I'm just fine," she lied. "And we have good news. I have the name of the mother and the child."

He stopped in his tracks. "That's great," he said, but his expression was unreadable. "Tell me more. Come sit by me."

No. She couldn't. Her mind and heart and body couldn't take being too near. Not in her present jittery state.

"I've been sitting awhile," she said. "Let me stand while I tell you."

He gave her a curt nod and advanced a step closer. Such a tiny step, but longing flooded her heart. She battled tears and found a smile. Not a convincing one, it seemed.

"You're distressed," he said, reaching out as if to touch her.

"No!" she said, rushing in to spare him from worrying. "I'm sorry. I'm just a bit tired." Lying was becoming such a bad habit. "No, the news is mostly good. The mother has been lurking on the board, so you and your condition were no surprise. She had plenty of time to ask questions of friends and professionals. She took her son for genetic testing. She checked you out thoroughly."

"The child?"

"No identifiable problems."

Jeremy closed his eyes. When he opened them again, he came right up to Eden and kissed her on the forehead. He folded her against his heart. "Thank goodness. Thank *you* for finding the truth."

Eden was struggling not to let Jeremy see how he affected her. She had to keep talking.

"The mother, Alisson August, knows who you are, but she doesn't want to meet you now," she said, pulling back in his arms to look at him. "She doesn't want assistance yet, but she sees the wisdom of keeping the door open. If things should change or if any new medical evidence should become available, she'd want to do something then."

Jeremy nodded. He released Eden and when they parted— "You crinkled," he said.

She remembered the papers she had been bringing him. She handed over a magnifier. "Alisson e-mailed me this."

Jeremy looked down at the woman and child on the page and froze. "He looks like me," he said.

"A lot," Eden agreed. "I think that's part of the reason Alisson wants to keep you a secret from him for now. She's afraid the resemblance will either scare him or make him want something he can't have. She's single."

They turned their attention to the woman, who was blond and ordinary yet very appealingly pretty. A quiet person, Alisson had said. Suddenly the truth dawned on Eden.

Jeremy could have a family if he wanted one. There was

no impediment because of his genetic material. This child was already here, already safe. This woman knew who he was and yet she wasn't crowding to get near him. She wouldn't be too demanding. She knew his situation and his condition and—

"She was glad you contacted her," Eden said. "She wasn't condescending or pitying or any of those things you don't like in a woman."

Jeremy frowned. "Eden?"

She bit her lip to keep it from trembling and struggled to find her voice. "You could have what you thought you never could have," she finally managed to say. "Without guilt." But her throat was closing up. Her eyes were burning. She couldn't continue.

Jeremy dropped the paper and gathered her close. "Don't," he said, thickly. "Don't cry."

"I'm not."

But of course she was. "I'm just so happy for you," she said. Another lie. "I want you to be happy. So much." Which was the complete truth and yet not the truth at all.

Because she wanted him to be happy *with her*. With Eden Byars. She wanted him to love her. She had, finally, done the most stupid thing she could ever do. She had given to Jeremy all she had to give. And now she had nothing to take away with her. And yet…

"Please be happy," she begged.

He kissed her slowly, carefully, her tears wetting her face.

"I will. You won't have to worry," he promised. "I don't want you to ever worry."

She nodded against his face. "I won't. I mean, I'll have so much to do when I get home. Getting my classroom ready. Researching my plans for the school. Getting together with friends I've missed." She stopped, unable to continue her lies or hold her smile. "I really have to go. The press conference is tomorrow. Mrs. Ruskin and I have some last-minute items to go over. She spoke to you earlier?"

"About the arrangement of the furniture to accommodate the crowd? Yes. I owe you two a debt of gratitude for thinking of that and letting me know the placement of everything. I need to come clean, but if it has to be done, I'd at least like to do it with some dignity. Admitting to the world that I have a disease is one thing. Letting them see me stumble is another. The last thing I want is for this to turn into a pity party. I don't want to be seen as weak."

"We'll run through a rehearsal tonight." But Jeremy wouldn't stumble, Eden knew. He'd gotten very good at this kind of thing. She was the one who had made mistakes. And yes, she might be a changed woman, a woman of confidence who ran toward adventure now when she had run from it in the past, but where Jeremy was concerned she had stumbled badly.

Tomorrow would be both the proudest day she could remember and a nightmare as well.

Eden tried to pretend that today was like any other, but her heart wasn't having any of it. Her bags were packed and there were only a few hours left before Cinderella's carriage turned back into a pumpkin.

"Don't get morose," she ordered herself. There were still those few hours left. Jeremy still needed her.

This gathering had turned into something bigger than

anticipated. Word had gotten out that Jeremy Fulton, who rarely spoke to the press, was having a big gathering and that the papers were invited. Suddenly people who hadn't been invited were calling to see if they could attend. A blurb snuck into a local paper, an Internet blog speculated on what could be so momentous that the head of the Fulton empire would bother to invite the press to his home.

Lula and Mrs. Ruskin had been forced to hire temps to help out, but at last everything seemed to be ready. The ballroom had been opened and arranged. Jeremy knew where everything was located. All that remained was for him to greet his guests, entertain them in that wonderful way he had and make a tasteful announcement about his condition, qualifying that with the fact that Fulton Enterprises was doing better than ever and so was the head of the company.

With a little luck the public would take the news in stride, Jeremy would see his guests out and then she and Jeremy would say their final goodbyes.

By tomorrow she would be back in St. Louis. *I'll be happy.* She forced the thought out. Jeremy needed a smiling, able assistant at his side tonight, not a woman in tears.

As if her thoughts had called him, the door to his room opened and he came down to the lobby where she was looking out the window.

"No curiosity seekers yet?" he asked with a grin.

She gave him a mock-stern look. "Don't be flippant. I know you'd rather be having all your teeth pulled than doing this."

Jeremy raised an eyebrow. "Well, that would get the press's attention, if I showed up without any teeth."

She bopped him on the arm. "Behave."

"Yes, teacher," he drawled. "And, Eden?" He leaned close, so close that his lips warmed her ear and sent a delicious shiver down her spine. "You and Mrs. Ruskin and Lula pulled off a coup. It was a good idea to make this more of a party than a mere press conference."

"That's because Mrs. Ruskin said that you look your best in a tux, a crisp white shirt and black bow tie. She was right."

A low growl escaped him and he leaned closer just as the doorbell rang.

"Receiving line, my lady," he said, offering his arm as Donald came in dressed in full formal butler garb. The older man gave Eden a wink.

"Places, everyone," Jeremy teased, but his arm was steely beneath Eden's palm. This could be the nightmare he had dreaded for so long. She intended to make sure that it wasn't.

An hour later, she decided that her fears had been misplaced. Jeremy had handled the entire affair with his usual charm and aplomb. He had made each woman who entered his house feel special and beautiful. He had made every man laugh.

"Fulton, you know how to throw a press conference. Great food, gorgeous women, good music. None of those dry-as-sawdust, stuffy affairs we're all used to," Jonathan DeFray said, pounding Jeremy on the back.

"We didn't want to put anyone to sleep," Jeremy said with an amused look.

"Fat chance of that. When a man goes to these lengths for what's supposed to be a press conference, I'll assume he's got something pretty important to announce. Everyone's holding their breath. What is it, Fulton? New project, something international? Have you come up with some new technology that will rock everyone's world?"

Again, Eden felt Jeremy tense beside her though his face and his demeanor betrayed none of that tension. "Nothing so exciting," he told Jonathan. Then he turned to Eden. "It's time."

She stood aside as he moved to the microphone. Her breath froze in her throat. If she could have taken his place, taken his condition in that moment, she would have.

"I've called you here tonight for a simple announcement," Jeremy said calmly. "Because I work with so many of you, you deserve to know that there's been a change in my life, but I want you to know that it's not a change that will affect our relationships. At least, I hope it won't."

A murmur went through the crowd.

Jeremy held up his hand. "In recent months, I've been diagnosed with a condition that's stealing my vision. In a few words, I'm slowly going blind."

A woman gasped. Jeremy paused as someone shushed her.

For a second Eden thought Jeremy looked toward her, but he quickly turned back to the crowd. He needed to do this alone. "I'm not sure how severe my blindness will be. At the moment it's only my central vision that's affected. But one thing I want to assure you, Fulton Enterprises is healthy and thriving and so am I. I have creative, accomplished employees, and we'll continue to grow and to thrive no matter my situation."

A silence fell on the room, and people began to shift on their feet. Jeremy turned to a woman perhaps six feet forward and to the right, in the perfect place for him to see the best. "I can still appreciate a gorgeous woman in a blue dress that matches her eyes, Loretta." He turned to his left, again searching for the person in perfect visual range. "And Geoffrey, I can still see that you insist on wearing that putrid green tie even though I've heard your wife complaining about it in the past."

A laugh went through the crowd, and the tension backed off a notch. Jeremy signaled to the musicians to start playing again. He signaled to Donald to clear the dance floor and the world seemed to breathe a collective sigh of relief.

Eden's knees threatened to give way. Jeremy caught her under the arm. "Are you all right?"

She looked up into his troubled eyes. "I'm wonderful. You were wonderful." *You always were,* she thought. "But you'd better see to your guests. A man can't drop a bomb-shell like that and not expect to field a few questions."

Jeremy frowned. "I wish—"

But a woman rushed up to him just then. "Jeremy, you gorgeous, scintillating man. You were always the most charming man in town. I want to hear more," she said, linking her arm through his.

Eden smiled at him and gave him a little wave. The crowd swallowed Jeremy and the woman up.

During the next half hour Eden watched him hold court. He dazzled the women; he amused and impressed the men. His news, and the fact that he seemed to still be functioning as always, endeared him to the crowd. For tonight it was enough. The secret was out and he had survived.

Tears of gladness clogged Eden's throat. Her vision

blurred. She turned away, and that was when she saw the woman standing just inside the door. Wearing a simple black dress. She was a stranger and yet not a stranger at all.

Eden came forward. "I thought you didn't want to meet him."

Alisson August shrugged self-consciously, her hair sliding over her shoulders with the movement. And Eden saw now that, contrary to her photo, there was nothing ordinary about this woman. She was a beauty, the rare kind, the kind that didn't need adornments to make her shine. "I saw the blurb in the newspaper. Curiosity won out. He was…he's brave, isn't he?" she asked.

Eden's throat closed up. She struggled for words. The right words. *She's the right one for him,* she couldn't help thinking. *She has his child. She fits. They share something. He could watch his son grow.* "He's brave and he's noble and a lot of other good things."

"That's good to know."

"He's an amazing, intelligent man, as well, and he has a wonderful sense of humor. He has a lot to offer the world."

The woman studied her, a slightly amused and sympathetic look on her face. "Eden, are you trying to convince *me,* or are you in love with him?"

Eden held back her gasp. Had she been so transparent? Obviously, yes. Did other people see what this woman saw? She prayed that they didn't. "Jeremy's been a very good employer, the best I've ever had, but I'm leaving. I have my own life."

And her job here was through, she realized. Staying longer wouldn't accomplish anything. If Alisson realized the truth, others might, too. And then Jeremy would know.

"You should go introduce yourself," she told Alisson. "He'd very much like to meet you, I'm sure."

The woman gazed at her for a minute as if trying to read her mind. Then she turned away in the direction of Jeremy.

The gears clicked into place. Everything here was done. The play had ended. There was no more.

Panic and tears threatened, and Eden escaped the room. She found Donald and made up some story about being called away for an emergency. She asked him to have someone bring down her bags and drive her to the train.

Then she turned back in search of Jeremy. He was in the middle of a crowd. People were laughing, joking with him. The women all looked as if they had bedrooms on their minds. Then she saw Alisson give her one last questioning look.

In a split second Eden made her decision. She gave Alisson a nod and she headed for the door. Leaving without saying goodbye was a completely cowardly thing to do. It was such a wrong way to end things, given all that happened here these past few months, but—

*If I stay, he'll know. He'll feel guilty and he'll hate himself, because I couldn't get through a goodbye without tears. Once I'm gone, I'll call or I'll send him a letter.*

It was all she could do. In time, Jeremy would forgive her for leaving so abruptly and ungraciously. His world would right itself. Everyone finally knew the truth and had accepted it. Alisson was so right for him. Eventually Jeremy would see that, too.

Eden closed her eyes. She did her best to steady herself. Then she fled.

\* \* \*

Jeremy was pleased at the results of this meeting, but he couldn't wait for it to be over. He'd barely gotten to talk to Eden all night and now…where was she, anyway?

He glanced around, cursing the blurry areas where he couldn't see clearly. Off to his right, a woman came into his field of vision. A small shock wave slipped through him but he quickly adjusted and decided that he wasn't all that surprised. In her circumstances, he might have shown up, too. The woman held out her hand. "We haven't met, but…"

"You're Alisson," he said.

She gave him a small smile. "And I'm clearly not really who you're looking for."

He frowned, not understanding. "I'm just a bit surprised to see you here."

She shrugged. "I'm a bit surprised to be here. I saw the announcement of the event and I just came to get a glimpse, but your secretary suggested that I come meet you."

"Eden?" The very sound of her name on his own lips had him glancing off to the side.

"I don't think she's in the room. I saw her leave."

Suddenly Jeremy felt tired. He'd accomplished his goals for the evening. He had only a short time left with Eden, but no one showed any signs of wanting to leave yet and…damn, where was she?

"This is probably not the best time for us to talk," Alisson said.

"Probably not, but we will, won't we? In time?"

"Yes, I think we have to, but…"

He blinked and looked at her. She seemed uncomfortable. "I'm involved with someone," she said.

Now Jeremy understood. "That's nice. You didn't think I had made plans for you, did you?"

She gave a self-conscious laugh. "Not exactly, but your secretary, Eden, was singing your praises to me so much that I wasn't sure what to think."

Ah. Jeremy remembered Eden's words. She was worrying about him again, trying to fix things for him again. When he spoke to her next, he'd have to set her straight. But she wasn't here.

He glanced around the room again, more urgently. Donald came into view. Jeremy could tell by his stance that something was bothering him.

"I don't mean to interrupt you, Mr. Fulton, but—"

"Tell me," Jeremy said. Donald didn't worry over trivial matters.

"She's gone." Donald blurted the words out. "Some emergency, she said. I just brought down her bags. One of the drivers is going to take her to the train. I thought you might want to know."

The noise of the room seemed to increase a hundred-fold. Jeremy's tie felt too tight, the room felt too crowded. And empty at the same time.

He struggled to control himself, to breathe, to think, to maintain the cool facade that had stood him in good stead all his life, the one that held his emotions in check. Eden was leaving. Now.

The words flayed him. He reminded himself that she wanted to leave. She'd come here because she needed money. She didn't need *him*.

But she was leaving without even saying goodbye. He had to get across the room. He had to find her, but chairs had shifted, people blocked his way. The paths they had laid out yesterday weren't clear anymore. He couldn't get across the room without exposing the physical reality of his limitations.

"It doesn't matter." He said the words almost violently, making Donald flinch.

"It doesn't matter what people think or what I can't do or see. Eden!" And with that, Jeremy rushed forward.

A crowd of people seemed to appear out of nowhere. He crashed into them, knocking drinks from their hands and ignoring their gasps.

The clock was ticking. Had the driver already pulled around? Had she already gone?

Without taking time to apologize, Jeremy ran on. A table banged his leg, and he stumbled to his knees. The sleeve of his jacket caught on something and tore. He flung it off and ran on.

"Eden, don't go," he called again. "Don't leave!"

He bumped a woman, and she shrieked. The crowd was starting to buzz. "What's wrong with him?" some man muttered. "He's gone mad."

"He can't see," someone else yelled.

Jeremy ignored them all. Finding Eden before she left was all that mattered. Somehow he located the front door and threw it open, rushing out into the night.

The crowd followed him into the dark, harsh whispers breaking the stillness.

And then he saw a figure that had to be her, moving away from him down the drive.

"Eden," he said, not a roar this time but a hoarse, anguished animal sound.

It was enough. She turned, she stopped. He rushed to her.

"You were leaving without a word," he said.

She bit her lip and nodded. "Yes." Her voice came out shaky.

Jeremy closed his eyes. "You didn't want to say goodbye."

"I—" She looked to the side. "I couldn't and—my work here is through. You've accomplished all you need to. Everything is settled. You're fine on your own."

*No, he would never be fine on his own. Not without her.* But could he say that? He couldn't try to hold her out of pity.

Suddenly she moved closer. "Jeremy, your jacket's gone. Your shirt is torn, your tie's askew and your hair—" She reached out and touched his hair. He thought he would die from the desire to reach out and pull her to him.

"He slammed into a few things trying to get to you," Jonathan said from somewhere off to the side. "He kept calling your name. He fell. More than once."

"Jeremy? You fell? Because of me. I'm sorry."

"Don't." He snapped the word out, his throat aching. "It doesn't matter. None of it. All my life I've built an impregnable wall around myself to hide my weaknesses and imperfections. And since my diagnosis I've hidden my condition. I presented an illusion to the world, and as long as I never let down my guard I could go on. Even tonight when I revealed the truth I was still playing a role, letting my pride dictate my actions. But…you were leaving and none of it mattered anymore."

"I couldn't stay," she said softly and there were tears in her voice. "I was afraid you would see how hard it was for me to leave you."

She was afraid of showing him how she felt? He knew that feeling. He needed to conquer his own tendency to hide his deepest thoughts, and yet…how could he tell her what he wanted to tell her? How could he ask for what he wanted?

He reached out and brushed his fingers over her cheeks and felt her tears.

"Eden, I hurt you once before when we were young. I know I did. And others have hurt you. I don't want to ever hurt you again. I don't want to cause you another moment of worry. And yet…"

She waited.

He, who had always known the right words, struggled for them now. His thoughts were a jumble. His heart pounded, and he fought for reason. This was Eden. She was his heart. The words he chose now were the most important he might ever speak.

*Let her go. Let her go,* he ordered himself. He'd brought her to tears, he thought, rage at himself sluicing through him.

And yet, he owed her the truth. The complete truth. Finally.

"I know you thought that Alisson and I might be a couple, but that's just not going to happen, Eden. Despite what you want for me, she and I aren't meant for each other. And…I've never ever loved a woman, so by rights I shouldn't even recognize the emotion. The truth is that I've always thought I was like my father, incapable of love, an emotion that seemed to wreck so many lives that I never wanted any part of it, but…you…your voice…it's what I listen for each day. Your touch is what I crave, your laughter makes my day complete. You've changed my world. I had to tell you that before you left. I—"

"Jeremy?" Eden said, her voice thick. She came closer. He felt her gaze full on him.

"I can't lie to you," he said. "I don't want you to go, and I'm going to be hell to live with without you. But the fact that I feel that way...none of it matters, because as much as I want to promise you everything any man promises a woman, the truth is that I don't know what the future holds for me. I can't ask anyone to share that future. All the money I have can't change things."

His voice trailed off. Eden was gazing at him. The crowd was completely hushed. He stood before the world, emotionally naked, and for the first time in his life, he didn't give a damn how the world saw him. Because his true world was Eden.

Eden could barely breathe, her heart was hurting so much. Jeremy was here, beside her. The things he had said...all the things he had said...

Was he offering...

No. *Don't hope,* she told herself. He had said things, wonderful things, but he'd offered nothing.

Still...had he said he loved her?

Yes, but there was love and there was love. Jeremy had had many short-term relationships. He'd probably used the word before, but he didn't have real relationships. He had told her that so many times.

She closed her eyes, confused and afraid. Her throat closed up. She fought tears. No more hiding from the truth, she told herself, even if the truth was humiliating.

"I don't know what you're offering or even if you're

offering anything at all, but I don't absolutely have to have children," she said. "Perfect DNA isn't a requirement, and all your money won't give me what I want, either."

He stood there looking down at her, looking like all she wanted in the world, all she would ever want.

She leaned forward. Jeremy reached out.

Then he stopped. "Tell me what you want," he said solemnly. "Tell me what you truly want and need."

Taking a breath she steeled herself. She fought not to lie, to give him the truth no matter how difficult this was for her. "It's always been you," she finally managed to say, her heart hurting, tears gathering. "I shouldn't even have come here at all, because deep in my heart, I knew that was true. I want you. I love you, Jeremy."

He closed his eyes. "You know that I'll never be a whole man," he said.

A laugh bubbled up. His eyes opened. "Jeremy, you're more of a man than I've ever met. You take chances. You help *me* take chances and challenge me to try new and exciting things, to push myself when I think I can't. You continue to do your job every day, even when it's a struggle. You're kind and smart. You help people and you make me laugh and…you're all I want."

"Eden…" Jeremy fell to his knees.

Instantly she remembered the crowd that was watching this man who had fought all his life for his pride. She remembered that people had said he had fallen several times when he was coming for her. His hand was bleeding. This man who was such a fighter that he never gave in to weakness, this man she loved…

Had he hit more than his hand? His head?

"Jeremy, what's wrong? Are you hurt? Let me see your hand." She dropped to her knees beside him and took his hand in hers.

He turned his head until they were nose to nose. "Eden," he whispered, ignoring their audience and kissing the side of her neck. "You're messing up my proposal, love."

Somewhere in the background someone chuckled, but Eden didn't care. She blinked and clutched Jeremy's hand so hard that he winced. "What?" she whispered.

He smiled at her, and her heart melted completely.

"You said you loved me," he told her.

"Yes."

"And I told you that you were the only woman I've ever loved."

He had, hadn't he?

"I thought maybe you were just trying to send me away without breaking my heart too badly. I know that you'd feel guilty if you thought you had hurt me," she said.

He caressed her cheek solemnly. "I would rather hurt myself than you. Any day, any time. You're the most precious thing in my world. But I wouldn't tell you I loved you if it weren't true." He kissed her, gently. "Will you marry me, Eden? Stay as long as you can?"

She frowned. "As long as I can, Jeremy?"

"I don't actually know what I'll eventually become or how great the difficulties will be. You might change your mind."

"Jeremy," Eden said, hitting him on the arm hard and frowning at him. "You either ask me for forever or you don't ask at all." She crossed her arms under her breasts.

The crowd cheered.

Jeremy ignored them. His grin was magic. It melted her fears completely. Her heart soared, and she couldn't help smiling back at him.

He took her hand and made her stand up while he knelt before her. "Eden, my first and only love, will you be my wife and the mother of any children we adopt no matter what comes?"

She tugged his hand until he was standing beside her. "Just try and get rid of me," she whispered. "I'll be your wife, your companion and your lover."

"I'll build your school," he promised, taking her in his arms.

"And I'll be your eyes, Jeremy," she whispered only to him. "You'll be my…everything."

Jeremy pulled her closer. "Who knew that what I thought was my life's biggest tragedy would bring me my greatest joy? Welcome home, love. I'm so sorry I messed up our first kiss years ago. What a blind man I was."

She laughed up at him. "That's all right, Jeremy. You can kiss me now. You can kiss me forever."

"What an absolutely fantastic idea," he said, sliding his fingers into her hair and covering her mouth with his own.

"Eden?" he said when they had come up for air.

"Yes?"

"Do you know what I can see when I'm kissing you?"

"Tell me," she whispered against his lips.

"I can see the future, and it's beautiful."

"I'm going to love being married to you," she said.

Jeremy let out a whoop and swung her around in his arms. "We need some music. Donald," he said to his friend and servant. "Tell the orchestra to come outside so that we can all dance under the stars. And tell the driver he can go home to his wife. We won't need him. She's staying. She's mine."

He turned to his guests. "I hope you'll help us celebrate the announcement of our engagement."

The crowd gave a cheer. "You two sure know how to hold a jaw-dropping press conference," Jonathan said. "You're my kind of people."

The two of them laughed and thanked him. "Don't they make a nice couple?" Eden heard someone ask. It sounded like Alisson.

"She must have had what he's been looking for all his life." That was unmistakably Miriam's voice.

Jeremy laughed. "She's right," he whispered to Eden. "I didn't see it right away, but now it's crystal clear."

Eden rose on her toes and kissed him as the orchestra began to play. "I'm so happy Ashley sent for me."

"The woman's a gem," he agreed. "We'll have to name our first child after her."

With a smile Eden moved into his arms and into the dance. Her heart had come home at last.

# MILLS & BOON®
*Pure reading pleasure*™

# SEPTEMBER 2008 HARDBACK TITLES

## ROMANCE

| | |
|---|---|
| **Ruthlessly Bedded by the Italian Billionaire** *Emma Darcy* | 978 0 263 20350 9 |
| **Mendez's Mistress** *Anne Mather* | 978 0 263 20351 6 |
| **Rafael's Suitable Bride** *Cathy Williams* | 978 0 263 20352 3 |
| **Desert Prince, Defiant Virgin** *Kim Lawrence* | 978 0 263 20353 0 |
| **Sicilian Husband, Unexpected Baby** *Sharon Kendrick* | 978 0 263 20354 7 |
| **Hired: The Italian's Convenient Mistress** *Carol Marinelli* | 978 0 263 20355 4 |
| **Antonides' Forbidden Wife** *Anne McAllister* | 978 0 263 20356 1 |
| **The Millionaire's Chosen Bride** *Susanne James* | 978 0 263 20357 8 |
| **Wedded in a Whirlwind** *Liz Fielding* | 978 0 263 20358 5 |
| **Blind Date with the Boss** *Barbara Hannay* | 978 0 263 20359 2 |
| **The Tycoon's Christmas Proposal** *Jackie Braun* | 978 0 263 20360 8 |
| **Christmas Wishes, Mistletoe Kisses** *Fiona Harper* | 978 0 263 20361 5 |
| **Rescued by the Magic of Christmas** *Melissa McClone* | 978 0 263 20362 2 |
| **Her Millionaire, His Miracle** *Myrna Mackenzie* | 978 0 263 20363 9 |
| **Italian Doctor, Sleigh-Bell Bride** *Sarah Morgan* | 978 0 263 20364 6 |
| **The Desert Surgeon's Secret Son** *Olivia Gates* | 978 0 263 20365 3 |

## HISTORICAL

| | |
|---|---|
| **Scandalous Secret, Defiant Bride** *Helen Dickson* | 978 0 263 20210 6 |
| **A Question of Impropriety** *Michelle Styles* | 978 0 263 20211 3 |
| **Conquering Knight, Captive Lady** *Anne O'Brien* | 978 0 263 20212 0 |

## MEDICAL™

| | |
|---|---|
| **Dr Devereux's Proposal** *Margaret McDonagh* | 978 0 263 19910 9 |
| **Children's Doctor, Meant-to-be Wife** *Meredith Webber* | 978 0 263 19911 6 |
| **Christmas at Willowmere** *Abigail Gordon* | 978 0 263 19912 3 |
| **Dr Romano's Christmas Baby** *Amy Andrews* | 978 0 263 19913 0 |

# MILLS & BOON®
## *Pure reading pleasure*™

## SEPTEMBER 2008 LARGE PRINT TITLES

### ROMANCE

| | |
|---|---|
| **The Markonos Bride** *Michelle Reid* | 978 0 263 20074 4 |
| **The Italian's Passionate Revenge** *Lucy Gordon* | 978 0 263 20075 1 |
| **The Greek Tycoon's Baby Bargain** *Sharon Kendrick* | 978 0 263 20076 8 |
| **Di Cesare's Pregnant Mistress** *Chantelle Shaw* | 978 0 263 20077 5 |
| **His Pregnant Housekeeper** *Caroline Anderson* | 978 0 263 20078 2 |
| **The Italian Playboy's Secret Son** *Rebecca Winters* | 978 0 263 20079 9 |
| **Her Sheikh Boss** *Carol Grace* | 978 0 263 20080 5 |
| **Wanted: White Wedding** *Natasha Oakley* | 978 0 263 20081 2 |

### HISTORICAL

| | |
|---|---|
| **The Last Rake In London** *Nicola Cornick* | 978 0 263 20166 6 |
| **The Outrageous Lady Felsham** *Louise Allen* | 978 0 263 20167 3 |
| **An Unconventional Miss** *Dorothy Elbury* | 978 0 263 20168 0 |

### MEDICAL™

| | |
|---|---|
| **The Surgeon's Fatherhood Surprise** *Jennifer Taylor* | 978 0 263 19974 1 |
| **The Italian Surgeon Claims His Bride** *Alison Roberts* | 978 0 263 19975 8 |
| **Desert Doctor, Secret Sheikh** *Meredith Webber* | 978 0 263 19976 5 |
| **A Wedding in Warragurra** *Fiona Lowe* | 978 0 263 19977 2 |
| **The Firefighter and the Single Mum** *Laura Iding* | 978 0 263 19978 9 |
| **The Nurse's Little Miracle** *Molly Evans* | 978 0 263 19979 6 |

# MILLS & BOON®
*Pure reading pleasure*™

# OCTOBER 2008 HARDBACK TITLES

## ROMANCE

| | |
|---|---|
| **The Greek Tycoon's Disobedient Bride** *Lynne Graham* | 978 0 263 20366 0 |
| **The Venetian's Midnight Mistress** *Carole Mortimer* | 978 0 263 20367 7 |
| **Ruthless Tycoon, Innocent Wife** *Helen Brooks* | 978 0 263 20368 4 |
| **The Sheikh's Wayward Wife** *Sandra Marton* | 978 0 263 20369 1 |
| **The Fiorenza Forced Marriage** *Melanie Milburne* | 978 0 263 20370 7 |
| **The Spanish Billionaire's Christmas Bride** *Maggie Cox* | 978 0 263 20371 4 |
| **The Ruthless Italian's Inexperienced Wife** *Christina Hollis* | 978 0 263 20372 1 |
| **Claimed for the Italian's Revenge** *Natalie Rivers* | 978 0 263 20373 8 |
| **The Italian's Christmas Miracle** *Lucy Gordon* | 978 0 263 20374 5 |
| **Cinderella and the Cowboy** *Judy Christenberry* | 978 0 263 20375 2 |
| **His Mistletoe Bride** *Cara Colter* | 978 0 263 20376 9 |
| **Pregnant: Father Wanted** *Claire Baxter* | 978 0 263 20377 6 |
| **Marry-Me Christmas** *Shirley Jump* | 978 0 263 20378 3 |
| **Her Baby's First Christmas** *Susan Meier* | 978 0 263 20379 0 |
| **One Magical Christmas** *Carol Marinelli* | 978 0 263 20380 6 |
| **The GP's Meant-To-Be Bride** *Jennifer Taylor* | 978 0 263 20381 3 |

## HISTORICAL

| | |
|---|---|
| **Miss Winbolt and the Fortune Hunter** *Sylvia Andrew* | 978 0 263 20213 7 |
| **Captain Fawley's Innocent Bride** *Annie Burrows* | 978 0 263 20214 4 |
| **The Rake's Rebellious Lady** *Anne Herries* | 978 0 263 20215 1 |

## MEDICAL™

| | |
|---|---|
| **A Mummy for Christmas** *Caroline Anderson* | 978 0 263 19914 7 |
| **A Bride and Child Worth Waiting For** *Marion Lennox* | 978 0 263 19915 4 |
| **The Italian Surgeon's Christmas Miracle** *Alison Roberts* | 978 0 263 19916 1 |
| **Children's Doctor, Christmas Bride** *Lucy Clark* | 978 0 263 19917 8 |

# MILLS & BOON®
*Pure reading pleasure™*

# OCTOBER 2008 LARGE PRINT TITLES

## ROMANCE

| | |
|---|---|
| **The Sheikh's Blackmailed Mistress** *Penny Jordan* | 978 0 263 20082 9 |
| **The Millionaire's Inexperienced Love-Slave** *Miranda Lee* | 978 0 263 20083 6 |
| **Bought: The Greek's Innocent Virgin** *Sarah Morgan* | 978 0 263 20084 3 |
| **Bedded at the Billionaire's Convenience** *Cathy Williams* | 978 0 263 20085 0 |
| **The Pregnancy Promise** *Barbara McMahon* | 978 0 263 20086 7 |
| **The Italian's Cinderella Bride** *Lucy Gordon* | 978 0 263 20087 4 |
| **Saying Yes to the Millionaire** *Fiona Harper* | 978 0 263 20088 1 |
| **Her Royal Wedding Wish** *Cara Colter* | 978 0 263 20089 8 |

## HISTORICAL

| | |
|---|---|
| **Untouched Mistress** *Margaret McPhee* | 978 0 263 20169 7 |
| **A Less Than Perfect Lady** *Elizabeth Beacon* | 978 0 263 20170 3 |
| **Viking Warrior, Unwilling Wife** *Michelle Styles* | 978 0 263 20171 0 |

## MEDICAL™

| | |
|---|---|
| **The Doctor's Royal Love-Child** *Kate Hardy* | 978 0 263 19980 2 |
| **His Island Bride** *Marion Lennox* | 978 0 263 19981 9 |
| **A Consultant Beyond Compare** *Joanna Neil* | 978 0 263 19982 6 |
| **The Surgeon Boss's Bride** *Melanie Milburne* | 978 0 263 19983 3 |
| **A Wife Worth Waiting For** *Maggie Kingsley* | 978 0 263 19984 0 |
| **Desert Prince, Expectant Mother** *Olivia Gates* | 978 0 263 19985 7 |